TOMMY SMITH'S ANIMALS

BY

EDMUND SELOUS

WITH EIGHT ILLUSTRATIONS BY
G. W. ORD

TWELFTH EDITION

CONTENTS

CHAP.		PAGE
I.	THE MEETING	1
II.	THE FROG AND THE TOAD	11
III.	THE ROOK	25
IV.	THE RAT	39
V.	THE HARE	54
VI.	THE GRASS-SNAKE AND ADDER	74
VII.	THE PEEWIT	96
VIII.	THE MOLE	115
IX.	THE WOODPIGEON	143
X.	THE SQUIRREL	166
XI.	THE BARN-OWL	187
XII.	THE LEAVE-TAKING	205

LIST OF ILLUSTRATIONS

	PAGE
"HE MAY HAVE FOUND ANOTHER HARE"	*Frontispiece*
"THAT IS WHY I AM SO WISE" . . .	9
"I SHALL KEEP AWAKE TILL THE RAT COMES"	39
PAT, PAT, PAT. "DO YOU HEAR?" . . .	41
"BITE HIM!"	51
"ALL HAPPY (EXCEPT THE HARE)" . . .	63
"THERE ARE THREE FROGS IN MY STOMACH AT THIS MOMENT"	79
"WE MOLES ARE VERY HEROIC" . . .	141

TOMMY SMITH'S ANIMALS

CHAPTER I.

THE MEETING

*'The owl calls a meeting, and has an idea:
They all think it good, though it SOUNDS rather queer."*

THERE was once a little boy, named Tommy Smith, who was very cruel to animals, because nobody had taught him that it was wrong to be so. He would throw stones at the birds as they sat in the trees or hedges; and if he did not hit them, that was only because they were too quick for him, and flew away as soon as they saw the stone coming. But he always *meant* to hit them—yes, and to kill them too,—which made it every bit as bad as if he really had killed them. Then, if he saw a rat, he would make his dog run after it, and if the poor thing tried to escape by running down a hole, he and the dog together would dig it out, and then the dog would bite it with his sharp teeth until it was quite dead. It never seemed to occur to this boy that the poor rat had done *him* no harm, and that it might be the father or mother of some little baby rats, who would now die of hunger. Even if the rat got away, he would whip the dog for not catching it, yet the dog had done his best; for, of course, dogs must do what their masters tell them, and cannot know any better. It was just the same with hares or rabbits, squirrels, rooks, or partridges. Indeed, this boy could not see any animal playing about, and doing no harm, without trying to frighten it or to hurt it.

When the spring came, and the birds began to build their nests, and to lay their pretty eggs in them, then it is dreadful to think how cruel this Tommy Smith was. He would look about amongst the trees and bushes, and when he had found a nest, he would take all the eggs that were in it, and not leave even one for the poor mother bird to sit on when she came back. Indeed, he would often tear down the nest too, after he had taken the eggs. Perhaps you will wonder what he did with these eggs.

THE MEETING

Well, when he had brought them home and shown them to his father and mother, who never thought of scolding him, or to his little brothers and sisters (for he was the eldest of the family), he would throw them away, and think no more about them. If he had left them in the nest, then out of each pretty little egg would have come a pretty little bird. But now, for every egg he had taken away, there was one bird less to sing in the woods in the spring and summer.

At last this boy became such a nuisance to all the animals round about, that they determined to punish him in some way or other. They thought the first thing to do was for all of them to meet together and have a good talk about it. In a wood, not far off, there was a nice open space where the ground was smooth and covered with moss. Here they all agreed to come one fine night, for they thought it would be nice and quiet then, and that nobody would disturb them, as, perhaps, they might do in the daytime.

So, as soon as the moon rose, they began to assemble, and I wish you could have been there too, to see them all come, sometimes one at a time, and sometimes two or three together.

The rat was one of the first to arrive, and then came the hare and the rabbit arm in arm, for they knew each other well, and were very good friends. The frog was late, for he had had a good way to hop from the nearest pond, where he lived, so that his cousin, the toad, who was slower, but lived nearer, got there before him. The snake had no need to make a journey at all, for he lived under a bush just on the edge of the open space. All the little birds, too, had gone to roost in the trees and bushes close by, so as to be ready in good time; and, when the moon rose, they drew out their heads from under their wings, and were wide awake in a moment. The rook and the partridge, and other large birds, were there as well, and the squirrel sat with his tail over his head, on the branch of a small fir tree. Then there were weasels, and lizards, and hedgehogs, and slow-worms, and many other animals besides.

In fact, if you had seen them all together, you would have wondered how one little boy could have found time to plague and

THE MEETING

worry so many different creatures. But you must remember that even a very *little* boy can do a *great* deal of mischief. Perhaps there were some animals there that little Tommy Smith had not hurt, because he had not yet seen them, but these came because they knew he *would* hurt them as soon as he could; and, besides, they were angry because their friends and companions had been ill-treated by him.

At last it seemed as if there was nobody else to come, and that everything was ready. Still, they seemed waiting for something, and all at once a great owl came swooping down, and settled on a large mole-hill which was just in the middle of the open space. Now, the owl, as perhaps you know, is a very wise bird, and, for this reason, all the other animals had chosen him to be the chief at their meeting, and to decide what was best to be done, in case they should not agree amongst themselves. He at once showed *how* wise he was, by saying that before he gave his own opinion he would hear what everybody else had to say. Then everybody began to talk at once, and there was a great hubbub, until the owl said that only one should speak at a time, and that the hare had better begin, because he was the largest of all the animals there.

So the hare stood up, and said he thought the best way to punish Tommy Smith was for every one of them to do him what harm he could. For his part, he was only a timid animal, and not at all accustomed to hurt people. Still, he had very sharp teeth, and he thought he might be able to jump as high as Tommy Smith's face and give him a good bite on the cheek or ear, and then run off so quickly that nobody could catch him. The rabbit spoke next, and said that he was just as timid as the hare, and not so strong or so swift. All *he* could do was to go on digging holes, and he hoped that some day Tommy Smith would fall into one of them. The hedgehog then got up, and said he would hide himself in one of these holes and put up his prickles for Tommy Smith to fall on. This would be sure to hurt him, and perhaps it might even put one of his eyes out. The rat thought it would be better if the hedgehog were to get into Tommy Smith's bed, so as to prick him all over when he was undressed; but the hedgehog would not agree to this, as he did not understand houses, and thought he would be sure to be caught if he went into one.

"Well, then," said the rat, "if you are afraid I will go myself, for I know the way about, and am not at all frightened. In the middle of the night, when it is quite dark, and when Tommy Smith is fast asleep, I will creep up the stairs and into his room, and then I can run up the counterpane to the foot of his bed and bite his toes."

"Why his toes?" said the weasel. "*I* can do much better than that, and if you will only show me the way into his room, I will bite the veins of his throat, and then he will soon bleed to death."

"That would be taking too much trouble," said the adder, coming from under his bush. "You all know that *my* bite is poisonous. Well, I know where this bad boy goes out walking, so I will just hide myself somewhere near, and when he comes by I will spring out and bite his ankle. Then he will soon die."

The birds, too, had different things to suggest. Some said they would scratch

Tommy Smith's face with their claws, and others that they would peck his eyes out. The frog wanted to hop down his throat and choke him, and the lizard was ready to crawl up his back and tickle him, if they thought *that* would do any good.

At length, when everyone else had spoken, the owl called for silence, and then he gave his own opinion in these words:—" I have now heard what every animal has had to say, and I have no doubt that we could easily hurt this boy very much, or perhaps even kill him, if we really tried to. But would it not be a better plan, first to see if we cannot make little Tommy Smith a better boy? Many little boys are unkind to animals because they know nothing about them, and think that they are stupid and useless. If they knew how clever we all of us really are, and what a lot of good we do, I do not think they would be unkind to us any more. I am sure that they would then have quite a friendly feeling towards us. But they cannot know this without being taught. Tommy Smith's father and mother *ought*, of course, to teach him, but as they will not do so, why should not

"THAT IS WHY I AM SO WISE"

we teach him ourselves? To do this, we shall have to speak to him in his own language, as he does not understand ours; but that is not such a difficult matter to us animals. I myself can speak it quite well when I want to, for I often sit on the trees near old houses at night, or even on the houses themselves, and I can hear the conversations coming up through the chimneys. That is why I am so wise. So I can easily teach all of you enough of it to make *you* able to talk to a little boy. My idea, then, is to *teach* little Tommy Smith before we begin to *punish* him, and it will be quite as easy to do the one as the other. Only let the next animal that he is going to kill or throw stones at, call out to him, and tell him not to do so. This will surprise him so much that he will be sure to leave off, and then each of us can tell him something about ourselves in turn. In this way he will get such a high idea of all of us, that he will never annoy us any more, but treat us with great respect for the future."

All the other animals thought this was a very clever idea of the owl's, and they agreed to do what he said, before trying anything else. So they begged him to begin teaching them the little-boy language at once (all except the rat, for he knew it too), so that they should lose no time. This the owl was quite ready to do, and he taught them so well, and they all learnt so quickly, that when little Tommy Smith got up next morning to have his breakfast, there was hardly an animal in the whole country that was not able to talk to him.

CHAPTER II.

THE FROG AND THE TOAD

*"Tommy Smith takes a turn in the garden next day,
And he finds the frog ready with something to say."*

AS soon as he had had his breakfast, Tommy Smith went out into the garden. It had been raining a little, and the first thing he saw was a large yellow frog sitting on the wet grass. Tommy Smith had a stick in his hand, and he at once lifted it up over his shoulder.

"Don't hit me," said the frog. "That would be a *very* wicked thing to do."

Tommy Smith was so surprised to hear a frog speak that he dropped his stick and stood with both his eyes wide open for several seconds.

"Why do you want to kill me?" said the frog.

Tommy Smith thought he must say something, so he answered, "Because you are a nasty, stupid frog."

"I don't know what you mean by calling me nasty," said the frog. "Look at my bright smooth skin, how nice and clean it is—cleaner than your own face, I daresay, although it is not long since you have washed it. As for my being stupid, you see that I can speak your language, although you cannot speak mine; and there are lots of other things which I am able to do, but you are not. I think I can catch a fly better than you can."

By this time it seemed to Tommy Smith as if it was quite natural to be talking to an animal, so he said, "I never thought that a frog could catch a fly."

"You shall see," said the frog. And as he spoke a fly settled on a blade of grass just in front of him. Then all at once a pink streak seemed to shoot out of the frog's mouth; back it came again —snap! His mouth, which had been wide open, was shut once more, and the fly was nowhere to be seen.

"Have you caught it?" said Tommy Smith.

"Yes," said the frog, "and swallowed it too."

"But how did you do it?" said Tommy Smith; "and what was that funny pink thing that came out of your mouth?"

THE FROG AND THE TOAD 13

"That was my tongue," the frog answered.

"Your tongue!" cried Tommy Smith. "But it looked so funny—not at all like my own tongue."

"No," said the frog. "My tongue is quite different to yours, and I do not use it in the same way. Hold out your hand so that I can hop into it, and then I will show you all about it."

Tommy Smith did as he was told, and —plop! there was the frog sitting in his hand. He at once opened his mouth, which was a very wide one, and allowed Tommy Smith to look at his tongue. What a funny tongue it was! It seemed to be turned backwards, for the tip, which was forked, instead of being just inside the lips as it is with us, was right down the throat, whilst the root of it was where the tip of our tongue is.

"But how do you use a tongue like that?" said Tommy Smith.

"Put the tip of your forefinger against your thumb," said the frog; "only, first, you must turn your hand so that the back of it is towards the ground, and the palm upwards." Tommy Smith did so.

"Now shoot your finger back as hard as you can." Tommy Smith did this too. "That," said the frog, "is the way I shoot my tongue out of my mouth when I want to catch a fly. Like this"— and he shot it out again. "You see it flies out like the lash of a whip, and my aim is so good that it always hits what I want it to, whether it is a fly or any other insect. Then I bring it back, just as you would bring your finger back to your thumb again, or as the lash of a whip flies back when you jerk the handle. The tip of it goes right down my throat where it was before, and the fly goes down with it."

"But why does the fly stay on your tongue?" said Tommy Smith. "Why doesn't it fly away?"

"It would if it could, of course," said the frog; "but it can't. My tongue, you see, is sticky—just feel it,—and so whatever it touches sticks to it, and comes back with it, if it isn't too large."

"Well, it is very curious," said Tommy Smith. "But when you said you could catch a fly, I did not know that you were going to eat it too. Then, do you like flies? and do you eat them every day?"

"I eat them when I can get them," said the frog; "but I like them better at night than in the daytime, if only I can catch them asleep. *You* eat during the day, and go to sleep at night. That is because you are a little boy. *I* am a frog, and we frogs like to be quiet in the daytime, and come out to feed when it is dark. We eat all sorts of insects—beetles, and flies, and moths, and caterpillars, and we eat slugs as well, and that is why we are so useful."

"Useful?" cried Tommy Smith. "Oh, I don't believe that! I am sure that a frog can be of no use to anybody."

"If you were a gardener you would think differently," said the frog; "at least, if you were not a very ignorant one. Have I not told you that I eat slugs and insects, and do you not know that slugs and insects eat the leaves of the flowers and vegetables in your garden? Have you never seen your father or his gardener pouring something over his rose-trees to kill the insects upon them? Now, I eat a great many insects in a single night, and I am only *one* of the frogs in your garden. There are others there besides me. If we were all to be killed, your father would find it much more difficult to have nice roses, and he would lose other flowers too, for there are insects which do harm to all of them. As for the slugs, if you will go out some night with a lantern, you may see them feeding on some of the handsomest plants, with your own eyes. That is to say, unless one of us frogs has been there; for if we have, you will not see any. Then you have seen caterpillars feeding on the cabbages. Well, *I* feed on those caterpillars. So always remember that the boy who kills a frog, does harm to his father's garden."

"I don't want to do that," said Tommy Smith; "so, if what you say is true"—

"You can find it in a natural history book, if you look," said the frog; "but I ought to know best myself. And I can tell you this, that when a frog speaks to a little boy, he always speaks the truth."

"Well, then," said Tommy Smith, "I will never hurt a frog again."

How pleased the poor frog was when he heard that. He gave a great hop out of Tommy Smith's hand, and came down upon the grass again, and then he hopped about for a little while, jumping higher each time than the time before. "Frogs always speak the truth," he said,—"when they speak to little boys. And now, perhaps, you would like to learn something more about me. Ask me any question you like, and I will answer it, because of what you have just promised."

This puzzled Tommy Smith a little, because he did not know where to begin, but at last he said, "You seem to me a very big frog. Were you always as big as you are now?"

"Why, of course not," said the frog, "a frog grows up just as much as a little boy does. I was once so small that you would hardly have been able to see me. But, besides being smaller, I was quite a different shape to what I am now. I had no legs at all, but instead of them I had a long tail, with which I used to swim about in the water, so that I was much more like a fish than a frog, and many people would have thought that I was a fish."

"That sounds very funny," said Tommy Smith.

"But were not you once much smaller than you are now?" said the frog.

"Oh yes!" Tommy Smith answered, "but however small I was, I was always a little boy, and had hands and feet, just as I have now."

"With you it is different," said the frog; "but there are some animals who are one thing when they are born, but change into another as they grow older. It is so with us frogs, and, if you listen, I will tell you all about it."

"Go on," said Tommy Smith, "I should like to hear very much."

"In the nice warm weather," the frog continued, "we hop about the country, and then we like to come into gardens. But in the winter we go to ponds and ditches and bury ourselves in the mud at the bottom, and go to sleep there. In the early spring, when the weather begins to get a little warmer, we come up again, and then the mother frog lays a lot of eggs, which float about in the water, and look like a great ball of jelly. After a time, out of each egg there comes a tiny little brown thing, and directly it comes out, it begins to swim about in the water, as well as if it had had swimming lessons, although, of course, it has never had any. It soon

THE FROG AND THE TOAD 19

grows bigger, and then you can see that it has a large round head and a long tail, but you cannot see any legs. But, as it goes on growing, a small pair of hind legs come out, one on each side of the tail, and then every day the tail gets smaller and the hind legs larger Still there are no front legs yet, but at last these come too. The tail is now quite short, and the head and body begin to look like a frog's head and body, which they did not do before, and they go on looking more and more like one, until, at last, the little brown thing with a tail, that swam about like a fish in the water, has changed into a little baby frog, that hops about on the land. Then this little baby frog grows larger and larger, until, at last, he becomes a fine fat frog, as big and as handsome as I am."

"It all seems very curious," said little Tommy Smith; "and I never knew anything about it before."

"That is because nobody ever told you," said the frog, "and you have never thought of finding out for yourself. But have you not passed by ponds in the spring time and seen those little brown things with tails that I have been telling you about, swimming about in them?"

"Oh yes, I have!" said Tommy Smith; "but I always thought that those were tadpoles."

"They are tadpoles," said the frog, "but they are young frogs for all that. A little tadpole grows into a big frog, just as a little boy grows into a big man. So you see, what a funny life mine has been, and what a lot of curious things have happened to me."

"Yes, you have had a funny life, Mr. Frog," said Tommy Smith, "and I think it is very interesting. But is there any other clever thing you can do besides catching flies? I can catch flies myself, but I do it with my hand instead of with my tongue."

"I can change my skin," said the frog, "and *that* is something which *you* cannot do."

"No," said Tommy Smith; "and I do not believe you can do it either. I think you are only laughing at me."

"Well," said the frog, "as it happens, my skin fits me quite comfortably now, and is not at all too tight, so I do not want to change it yet. But I have a cousin—a toad—who is quite ready to have a new one. He lives a little way off, in the shrubbery; so if you would like to see how he does it, I can bring you to him. He is very good natured, like myself, and if you will only promise to leave off hurting him, as well as me, he will be very pleased to show you, I am sure. I must tell you, too, that he is almost as useful in a garden as I am, for he lives on the same things, and catches flies and slugs just as I do."

"Then isn't he *quite* as useful?" said Tommy Smith; but as the frog didn't seem to hear, he went on with—"Then I will not hurt him any more than I will you."

"Come along, then," said the frog; and he began to hop in front of the little boy until they came to the shrubbery, where, in the mould beside a laurel bush, there sat a great, solemn-looking toad.

"I have brought someone to see you," said the frog. "This is little Tommy Smith, who used to be such a bad boy, and kill every animal he saw; but now he has promised not to hurt either of us."

"I am glad to hear it," answered the toad, "and I hope he will soon learn to leave other creatures alone too. Well, what is it he wants?"

"He wants to see you change your skin," said the frog.

"He had better look at me, then," said the toad, "for that is just what I am doing."

Tommy Smith bent down to look, and then he saw that the toad was wriggling about in rather a funny way, as if he was a little uncomfortable. He noticed, too, that his skin had split along the back, and it seemed to be wrinkling up and getting loose all over him, although it had been too tight before. This loose skin was dirty and old-looking, but underneath it, where it was split, Tommy Smith could see a nice new one that looked ever so much better. The more the toad wriggled, the looser the old skin got, and it was soon plain that he was wriggling himself out of it, just as you might wriggle your hand out of an old glove. At last he had got right out of it, and there lay the old skin on the ground.

"You see," said the frog, "that is how

we change our skin, just as you would change a suit of clothes. Does he not look handsome in his new one?"

"Very handsome—for a toad," said Tommy Smith. (The toad only heard the first two words of this, so he was *very* pleased.) "But what is he doing with his old skin, now that he has got it off?"

"If you wait a little, you will see," said the frog.

All this time the toad was pushing his old skin backwards and forwards with his two front feet, and he kept on doing this until, at last, he had rolled it up into a sort of ball. Then all at once he opened his great wide mouth and swallowed the ball, just as if it had been a large pill.

Tommy Smith was so surprised that he could hardly believe his eyes. "He has swallowed his own skin!" he cried.

"Of course I have," said the toad; "and the best thing to do with it, *I* think. I always like to be tidy, and not to leave things lying about. Now, good-morning," and he began to crawl away, for he was not an *idle* toad, but had business to attend to.

"And I have something to see about,"

said the frog, "so I will say good-bye, too, for the present. But remember what you have promised—never to hurt a frog or a toad;" and, with two or three great hops, he was out of sight.

Tommy Smith stood thinking about it all for some time, and then he ran into the house to tell everybody all the wonderful things he had learnt about frogs and toads, and to beg them never to kill any, because they do good in the garden.

CHAPTER III.

THE ROOK

*"The rook gives advice which we must not neglect.
I hope that his CAWS will produce an effect."*

IT was a nice, fine afternoon, and Tommy Smith was just going out for a little walk. He thought he would take his little terrier dog with him, so he called, "Pincher! Pincher!" But Pincher was not there, so he had to go without him. He was very sorry for this, for when he had got a little way from the house, what should run across the road but a rat, which sat down just inside the hedge and looked at him. "What a pity," he said out loud. "It's no use my trying to catch him alone, for he's sure to get away; but if Pincher had been with me, we would have hunted him down together."

"Then you would have done very wrong," said the rat, as he peeped at little Tommy Smith through the hedge. "You are a naughty boy yourself, and you teach Pincher to be a naughty dog."

"What!" said Tommy Smith; "then can you talk as well as the frog and toad?"

"Of course I can," the rat answered; "and I think if I were to talk to you for a little while as they did, you would not wish to hurt *me* any more either. I am sure I am just as clever as a frog or a toad."

"Can you change your skin like them?" said Tommy Smith.

"*My* skin never wants changing," said the rat; "but there are many other things I can do which are quite as clever as that."

"Well, do some of them," said Tommy Smith.

"I will," said the rat, "but not now. I can do things much better at night, and I prefer being indoors. To-night, when everybody is in bed and asleep, and the house is quiet, I will come to your room and wake you up. We can talk without being disturbed then, and I will soon teach you what a clever animal I am."

"I wonder what you will have to tell me," said Tommy Smith. "But say what you will, I believe that rats were only made to be killed."

The rat looked *very* angry. "They have

as much right to be alive as little boys have," he said. "But good-bye for the present," and he scampered away.

Tommy Smith walked on, and when he had gone some little way, he saw a number of rooks walking about a field. There was a haystack in the field, and he thought that perhaps if he were to get behind it and wait there for a little while, some of the rooks would come near enough for him to throw a stone at them. So he put several stones in his pocket, and then, with one in his hand, he began to walk towards the haystack. When he got there, he sat down behind it, and peeped cautiously round the corner. Yes, the rooks were still there, and some of them were coming nearer. "Oh," thought Tommy Smith (but I think he must have thought it aloud), "I have only to wait a little while, and then, perhaps, I shall be able to kill one."

"For shame!" said a voice close to him.

Tommy Smith looked all about, but he saw no one. "Who was that?" he said.

"Oh, fie!" said the voice. "What? kill a poor rook? What a wicked, wicked thing to do!"

Tommy Smith thought that there must be someone on the other side of the haystack, so he went there to see; but he found no one. Then he walked all round it, but nobody was there. But the rooks had seen him as he went round the haystack, and they all flew away. Then the same voice (it was rather a hoarse one) said, "Ah! now they are gone; so you will not be able to kill any of them."

"Who are you?" said Tommy Smith. "I hear you, but I cannot see anybody;" and, indeed, he began to feel rather frightened.

"If I show myself, will you promise not to hurt me?" said the hoarse voice.

"Yes, I will," said Tommy Smith.

"Very well, then. Throw away that stone you have in your hand, and the ones in your pocket as well."

Tommy Smith did this, and then, what should he see, standing on the very top of the haystack, but a large black rook. "Why, where were you?" he said. "I did not see you there when I looked."

"No," the rook said; "I hid myself under a little loose hay, for I did not want a stone thrown at me. I saw you coming, and I knew very well what you wanted to do, so I thought I would wait till you came,

THE ROOK

and then give you a good talking to. And, indeed, a naughty boy like you, who wants to kill rooks, *ought* to be scolded."

"I don't see why it is so naughty," answered Tommy Smith; "I have always thrown stones at the rooks, and nobody has ever told me not to."

"That is just why *I* have come to tell you how wrong it is," said the rook. "Would you like anybody to throw stones at you?"

Tommy Smith had to confess that he would not like *that* at all.

"Then, do you not know," the rook went on, looking very grave, "that you ought to do the same to other people that you would like other people to do to you? Have not your father and mother taught you that?"

"Oh yes, they have," said Tommy Smith; "but I don't think they meant animals."

"They ought to have meant them," said the rook, "whether they did or not, for animals have feelings as well as human beings. If you are kind to them, they are happy; but if you are unkind to them and hurt them, then they are unhappy. An animal, you know, is a living being like yourself, and surely it is better to make any living being happy than to make it unhappy."

Tommy Smith looked rather ashamed when he heard this, and did not quite know what to say. He thought the rook spoke as if he were preaching a sermon, and then he remembered having heard some old country people talk of "Parson Rook." Still, what he *said* seemed to be sensible, and all *he* could say, at last, as an answer was, "Oh, it's all very well, but you know you rooks do a great deal of harm."

"That shows how little you know about us," answered the rook. "We do not do harm, but good; and if the farmers knew how much good we did them, they would think us their best friends."

"Why, what good *do* you do them?" said Tommy Smith. "I always thought that you ate their corn."

"Perhaps we may eat a little of it," the rook said; "that is only fair, for if it were not for us, the farmer would have very little corn or anything else. I am sure, at least, that he would have scarcely any potatoes."

"Oh! but why wouldn't he?" said Tommy Smith.

THE ROOK

"I will explain it to you," said the rook. "So now listen, because you are going to learn something. There is an insect which you must often have seen, for it is very common in the spring-time. It is about the size of a very large humble-bee, and it has wings too, but you would not think it had at first, for they are hidden under a pair of smooth, brown covers, which are called shards. In the daytime it sits upon a tree or a bush, or sometimes you may see it crawling along a dusty road. But in the evening it begins to fly about with a humming noise. This insect is called the cockchafer. The mother cockchafer lays her eggs in the ground, and, after a few weeks, there comes out of each egg something which you would not think was a cockchafer at all, because it is so different. It has a yellow head and a long white body, which is bent at the end in the shape of a hook. On the front part of its body it has three pairs of legs, like a caterpillar's, only they are very small; but behind, it has no legs at all. It has a very strong pair of jaws, and with these it cuts through the roots of the grass and corn and wheat under which it lies, for these are the things on which it feeds. There is hardly anything which the farmer plants, and would like to see grow, that this grub or caterpillar (for that is what it is) does not eat and destroy; but what it likes best of all is the potato.

"The cockchafer-grub lies in the ground for four years before it turns into a real cockchafer, and all this time it keeps growing larger and larger; and, of course, the larger it grows, the more it eats and the more harm it does. Now if there were no one to kill this great, greedy thing, I don't know what the farmers would do, for all their crops would be spoilt. But we rooks kill them, and eat them too, for they are very nice, and we like them very much. We eat them for breakfast, and dinner, and supper, so you can think what a lot of them we eat in the day. When you see us walking about over the fields, we are looking for these great white things, and, whenever we give a dig into the ground with our beaks, you may be almost sure that we have either found one of them or something else which does harm too. When the fields are ploughed, a great many grubs and worms are turned up by the ploughshare, and then you may see us following the plough, and walking along in the furrow it has made, so as to pick up all we can get. So think what a lot of good we must do, and remember that the boy who kills a rook is doing harm to somebody's corn, or wheat, or potatoes."

"I do not want to do that," said Tommy Smith.

"Of course not," said the rook; "so you must not throw stones at us any more."

"I won't, then," said Tommy Smith. "But why do the farmers shoot you, if you do them so much good?"

"You may well ask," the rook answered. "They ought to be ashamed of themselves. I will tell you something about that. Once upon a time some farmers thought they would kill us all because we stole their corn; so they all went out together with their guns, and whenever they saw any of us, they fired at us and killed us, until, at last, there was not a rook left in the whole country; for all those that had not been shot had flown away. The farmers were so glad, for they thought that next year they would have a much better harvest. But they were quite wrong, for, instead of having a better harvest, they had hardly any harvest at all. The slugs and the caterpillars, and, above all, the great, hungry cockchafer-grubs, had eaten almost everything up; for, you see, there were no hungry rooks to eat *them*. The little corn we used to take from the farmers they could very well have spared, but now, without us, they found that they had lost much more than they could spare. Then the farmers saw how foolish they had been, and they were very sorry, and did all they could to get the rooks to come back again; and when they did come back, they took care not to shoot them any more."

Tommy Smith was very interested in this story which the rook told him, and he was just going to ask where it all happened, and whether it was near where he lived or a long way away, when the rook said, "Well, I must be flapping" (just as an old gentleman might say, "Well, I must be jogging"); "there is a meeting this afternoon which I ought to attend."

"A meeting!" Tommy Smith said, feeling quite surprised.

"Certainly," replied the rook. "Why not? I belong to a civilised community, so, of course, there are meetings. I should be sorry not to go to *some* of them."

It seemed very funny to Tommy Smith that birds should have meetings as well as men. "But, perhaps," he thought, "it is not quite the same kind of thing." Only he didn't like to *say* this, in case the rook should be offended, so he only asked, "What sort of a meeting is it that you are going to, Mr. Rook?"

"A very important one," the rook answered. "It is a meeting to try someone who is accused of having done something wrong."

"Why, then, it is a trial," said Tommy Smith. "But do rooks have trials?"

"Of course," said the rook. "Have I not just said that we are a civilised community? We are not *wild* birds. Amongst civilised people, when someone is accused of doing wrong, he is tried for it, is he not?"

"Oh yes!" said Tommy Smith. "If he is a man, he is."

"If he is a man, men try him," said the rook; "but if he is a rook, rooks do."

"But what do you do if you find him guilty?" said Tommy Smith.

"Why, we punish him, to be sure," said the rook; "and if he has been *very* wicked, we peck him to death."

"Oh, but that is very cruel," said Tommy Smith. He forgot that he had seen *innocent* rooks *shot* without thinking it cruel at all.

"Not more cruel than hanging a man," the rook answered. "Do you think it is?" and Tommy Smith couldn't say that he did. He thought he would very much like to see this trial that the rook was going to. "Oh, Mr. Rook," he said, "do let me go with you." But the rook said, "Oh no! that would never do. No men are allowed at our trials. There are no rooks at yours, you know."

"No," said Tommy Smith; "but that is because"—

"Never mind why it is," interrupted the rook; "no doubt there is some good reason, and we have our reasons too. We could not try a rook properly if we thought a man was watching us. It would make us nervous. Sometimes (but not very often) a man has watched us without our knowing it, and then he has told everybody about our wonderful trials. But people have not believed him; and other men, who sit at home and see very little, and only believe what they see, have written to say it was all nonsense. But now, when they tell *you* it is all nonsense, *you* will not believe *them*, because a rook himself has told you it is all true."

"Oh yes, and I believe it," said Tommy Smith. "But do tell me what the rook you are going to try has done."

"I cannot tell you that till we have tried him," said the rook, "for perhaps it may not be true after all. As yet, I do not even know what he is accused of. Perhaps it is of stealing the sticks from another rook's nest to make his own with. Perhaps it is of something even worse than that. But this you may be sure of, that if we *do* peck him to death, it will be because he has behaved himself in a manner totally unworthy of a rook. Now I really must go, or I shall be late. Good-bye,—and, let me see, I think you promised never to throw stones at rooks again."

"Oh no!" said Tommy Smith, "I promise not to."

"Or to shoot us when you grow up," said the rook, just turning his head round as he was preparing to fly.

"Oh no! indeed, I won't," said Tommy Smith; and the rook flew away with a loud caw of pleasure.

"I SHALL KEEP AWAKE TILL THE RAT COMES"

CHAPTER IV.

THE RAT

*"The rat is a king. Tommy Smith has a peep
At his palace: but is he awake or asleep?"*

"I SEE you," said the rat, as Tommy Smith passed through the yard of his father's house. "I see you, but it is not the right time yet. Wait till to-night."

So all that day Tommy Smith kept thinking of what the rat had promised; and when his bedtime came, instead of wanting to stay up longer, as he usually did, he was quite pleased to go, and went upstairs without making any fuss. "Now," thought he, as he made himself nice and snug in bed, "I shall keep awake till the rat comes. I am not at all sleepy. I can see the branch of the cedar tree by the window shaking in the wind, and I can hear the clock ticking on the staircase. 'Tick, tick—tick, tick,'— I wonder if it gets tired of saying that all day long, and all night long, too, without ever once stopping,—unless they don't wind it up. 'Tick, tick—tick, tick.' If I keep on counting it, I shan't go to sleep. 'Tick, tick—tick, tick—tick, tick—tick—squeak!'"

"What was that?" said Tommy Smith, as he sat up in bed. "That wasn't the clock;" and then, all at once, the old clock on the stairs struck one. "One? Then it must be wrong. When I got into bed it was only"—

"It is quite right," said a squeaky little voice close to Tommy Smith's ear. "I don't know what time it was when you got into bed, but you have been asleep for a good many hours; and now it is one in the morning, which is what *I* call a nice, comfortable time."

"I suppose you are the rat," said Tommy Smith, rubbing his eyes.

"Yes, I am," the same voice answered. "But it is too dark for you to see me here. Get up, and put on some of your clothes, and then we will come down to the kitchen. The fire is not quite out, and you can put a few more sticks on it. Then you will be able to see me as well as I can see you now, and we can talk together comfortably."

But can you see in the dark?" said Tommy Smith, whilst he sat on the bed and began to put on his stockings.

"Oh yes," the rat answered; "just as well as I can in the light."

"I wish I could," said Tommy Smith, "for I can't see *you* at all."

"Of course not," said the rat. "So, you see, it has not taken a *very* long time to find out something which I can do, but you can't. Well, you are ready now, so come along. You will be able to follow me, for I will pat the floor just in front of you with my tail,—and that is another thing which you couldn't do, even if you were to try for a very long time."

"Because *I* haven't got a tail," said Tommy Smith.

"That is one reason," the rat answered; "but you can't be sure you could do it even if you had one. It might be too short, you know. Now, come along." Pat, pat, pat. "Do you hear?"

Tommy Smith heard quite plainly, and he followed the rat through the door, and down the stairs, and right into the kitchen. The fire was still alight, as the rat had said.

There were some sticks lying in the fender, and Tommy Smith put some of them on to make it burn up. Then there was a blaze of light, and he could see the rat sitting up on his hind legs, and holding his front paws close to the bars so as to warm them.

"Now," the rat said, "we will begin at once. I promised to show you that I could do some clever things as well as the frog and toad. Do you see that bottle of oil standing there on the dresser?"

"Oh yes, I see it," said Tommy Smith.

"Well," the rat went on, "I should like to taste a little of it. But how do you suppose I am to get at it?"

"Why, by knocking it over," said Tommy Smith at once. "That is the only way that I can see."

"Fie!" said the rat. "That may be *your* way of drinking oil, but *I* should be ashamed to make such a mess. *I* am a rat, and I like to do things in a proper manner."

Tommy Smith felt a little offended at this, and he said, "I never knock a bottle over when I want to get oil or anything else out of it, for *I* am a little boy, and

THE RAT

have a pair of hands to lift it up with, and pour what is in it out of it. But you have no hands, and you cannot get your head into it, because the neck is too narrow, and your tongue is not long enough to reach down to where the oil is. So I don't see what you can do, unless you knock it over."

"Fie!" said the rat again. "Well, you shall soon see what I can do." And almost as he said this, he was on the dresser, and from there he gave a little jump on to the window-sill, and sat down, with his long tail hanging over the edge of it. Now the neck of the bottle came almost up to the edge of the window-sill, and the rat's tail was as long as the bottle.

"Oh, I see!" cried Tommy Smith.

"You will in a minute," said the rat, and he drew up his tail, and began to feel about with the tip of it till he had got it right inside the mouth of the bottle. Then he let it down again until it was dipped more than an inch deep into the oil at the bottom—for the bottle was not quite half full.

"Oh, how clever!" cried Tommy Smith, clapping his hands.

"I should think so," said the rat, as he drew out his tail, and then, putting the end of it to his mouth, he began to lick off the delicious oil. "You say that I have not a pair of hands," he went on. "That is true, but you see I have a tail, and I make it do just as well."

"So you do," said Tommy Smith; "and I see that you are a very clever animal indeed."

"We are clever in many other ways besides that," said the rat. "Oil, you know, is not the only thing which we care about. We like eggs for breakfast, just as much as you do, and when we find any, we take them to our holes, even if they are a long way off. Now, how do you think we do that?"

"Let me see," said Tommy Smith. "You have no hands, and I don't think you could carry an egg in your tail. I think you must push it in front of you with your nose and paws."

"Oh, we can do that, of course," said the rat, "but it takes so long, and, besides, the eggs might get broken. We have better ways than that. Sometimes, if there are a great many of us, we all sit in a row, and

THE RAT

pass the eggs along from one to the other in our fore-paws. But we have another way which is cleverer still, and as there is a basket of eggs in that cupboard there, I don't mind showing it you; for, between ourselves, when we do *that* trick, we like to have a little boy in the kitchen at nights to look at us. But, first, I must call a friend of mine." The rat then gave rather a loud squeak, and out another rat came running; but Tommy Smith didn't see where it came from.

"What is it?" said the second rat.

"Oh, I want to show little Tommy Smith how we carry eggs about," said the first rat.

"Very well," said the second rat. "Come along." And they both scampered into the cupboard together. (The door of the cupboard was half open. *I* think it ought to have been shut.)

Very soon the two rats came out again, but whatever do you think they were doing? Why, one of them was on his back, and the other one was dragging him along the floor by his tail, which he had in his mouth. But what was that white thing which the rat who was being dragged along was holding? Was it an egg? Yes, indeed it was; and he was holding it very tightly with all his four feet, so that it was pressed up against his body, and didn't slip at all.

Tommy Smith could hardly believe his eyes. "Is that how you do it?" he cried. "I see. One rat holds the egg, and the other pulls him along by the tail."

"Of course he does," said the rat. "He pulls him and the egg too."

"*Well*," Tommy Smith said, "of all the clever things I have *ever* seen, I think that is the cleverest. But where are you going with it?"

Yes, it was easy to ask, but there was no one to answer him; for both the little rats were gone all of a sudden,—and, what is more, the egg was gone too. "That will be one egg less for breakfast," thought Tommy Smith to himself. "I wonder that I didn't think of that before. Ah, Mr. Rat," he called out, "you may be very clever, but you are a thief, for all that. That egg which you have just taken away belongs to me. I mean it belongs to my father and mother. I call that stealing."

"Oh, do you?" said the rat, for he had

come out of his hole again. "Then just let me ask you one question. Who laid that egg?"

"Why, the hen did, of course," answered Tommy Smith.

"Oh, did she?" said the rat. "Then I suppose your father, or someone else, took it away from her, and *I* call *that* stealing."

"Oh no," said Tommy Smith; "I don't think it is."

"Don't you?" said the rat. "Well, you had better ask the hen what *she* thinks. I feel sure she would agree with me."

Tommy Smith felt certain that the rat was wrong, and that the egg had not been stolen. Still, he thought he had better not ask the hen; and, whilst he was considering what he should say, the rat went on with—
"There are other things we rats do which are quite as clever as what you have just seen. But, perhaps, if I were to show them you, you would make some other rude remark about stealing."

"Perhaps I should," Tommy Smith answered; "and, besides, I feel very sleepy, and should like to go upstairs to bed again."

As he said this, he yawned, and looked

straight into the fire; but, dear me, what *was* happening there? The coals in it seemed to be getting larger and larger, till they looked like the sides of great red mountains, and the spaces between them were like great caves, so deep that Tommy Smith could not see to the bottom of them. In and out of these caves, and all down the sides of the red mountains, hundreds of rats were running, and they all met each other in the centre of—what? Not of the fireplace. Of course not, for they would have been burnt. Nor of the kitchen either. There was no kitchen now. It had all disappeared. It was in the centre of a great hall, or amphitheatre, that Tommy Smith stood now; and when he looked round him, he saw only those great rugged mountains, which seemed to make its walls on every side. He looked up but he could see nothing. There was neither sun, nor moon, nor stars, yet everything was lit up with a strange light, which seemed to Tommy Smith like the red glow of the fire, though he couldn't see the fire any more. It had gone with the kitchen.

"Where am I?" he cried.

THE RAT

"In the great underground store-cupboard of the rats," said a voice close beside him; and, looking round, he saw the same rat who had come up into his bedroom, and taken him down to the kitchen, and shown him his clever tricks.

Yes, he was the same rat,—but how different he looked! On his head was a yellow crown, which was either of gold, or *else* it must have been cut out of a cheese-paring; and in his right fore-paw he held his sceptre, which looked *exactly* like a delicate spring-onion. He had a necklace of the finest peas round his neck, from which a lovely green bean hung as a pendant upon his breast, and his tail was twisted into beautiful *rings*. "I am the king of the rats," he said, "and all the other rats are my subjects. Those great caves which you see in the sides of the mountains are so many passages that lead into all the kitchens of the world. Through them we bring all the good things that we find in the kitchens, and larders, and pantries, and then we feast on them here in our own palace; for a rat's palace is his store-cupboard. See!" And with this the rat king struck his sceptre on the ground, and at once all the rats left off scampering about, and formed themselves into a great many long lines, which stretched from the mouths of all the caves right into the very middle of that wonderful place. There they all sat upright, side by side, waiting to be told what to do. Then the king of the rats waved his sceptre three times round his head, and called out, "Supper." Immediately all kinds of things that are good for rats to eat, such as bits of cheese, scraps of bread or toast, beans, onions, bacon, potatoes, apples, biscuits,—everything of that kind that you can possibly think of (besides *some* things that you *can't* possibly think of), began to pour out from all the great caves, and to fly like lightning from rat to rat down all the long lines. One rat seized something in his fore-paws and passed it on to another, and that one to the next, so quickly that it made Tommy Smith quite giddy to look at it; and he hardly knew what was happening, till all at once there was an immense heap of provisions piled up in the very centre of the floor. Then the king of the rats climbed up to the top of the heap, and called out, "Take your places," and in

"BITE HIM!"

THE RAT

a moment all the other rats came scampering up, and sat in a large circle round the great heap of provisions. "Begin!" said the king; and every rat made a leap forward, and fixed his teeth into the first piece of bread, or cheese, or toast, or bacon, that he could get hold of, and there was *such* a noise of nibbling, and gnawing, and scratching, and squeaking. Tommy Smith was quite frightened, and put his fingers to his ears.

"What are you doing that for?" said the king of the rats. "Didn't you hear me tell you to begin?"

"But I don't want to begin," said Tommy Smith.

"Why not?" said the king; and all the other rats stopped eating, and said, "Why not?"

"Because I don't like eating in the night," Tommy Smith answered; "and, besides, I can't eat what rats eat."

At this there was a great commotion, and the king of the rats cried out, "Bite him!" in a very loud and shrill voice.

Oh, how fast little Tommy Smith ran! "The caves!" he thought. "They lead to all the kitchens of the world, so one of them must lead to ours." He got to one, but the rats were close behind him. He could see their eyes shining in the dark as he looked back. "Oh dear!" he said; "I shall be caught. It's getting narrower and narrower, and, of course, it must be a rat's hole at the other end. Ah, there! I'm stuck, and I shall be bitten all over." As he said this, he kicked and squeezed as hard as he could, and, to his great surprise, he found that the sides of the rat-hole were quite soft—in fact, they felt very like bed-clothes; and the next moment his head was on his own pillow, and the old clock on the staircase struck two.

"Well, good-night," said a squeaky little voice, that he seemed to have heard before. "If you *will* go to sleep, I can't help it, but I think the way in which little boys turn night into day is quite dreadful."

The next time Tommy Smith heard the old clock on the stairs, it was striking eight, so, of course, it was broad daylight, and high time to get up. "What a funny dream I have had," he said, as he rubbed his eyes; "or did the rat really come, as he said he would?" Then, after thinking a little, he said to himself, "Rats are certainly very clever animals, and I don't think I'll kill another, even if they do steal a few things. At anyrate, *I* won't hurt *them* until *they* hurt *me*."

CHAPTER V.

THE HARE

*'When you've read through this chapter, I'm sure you'll declare
That you hate everybody who hunts the poor hare.'*

WHAT a beautiful day it was! How bright the sun shone, and how pleasantly the birds were singing,—for it was the lovely season of spring. All the air was full of melody, so that it seemed to Tommy Smith as if he had somehow got inside a very large musical box, which *would* keep on playing. And so he had, *really*, only it was Nature's great musical box,—the music was immortal, and the works were alive.

Far up in the sky the lark was doing his very best to please little Tommy Smith and everybody else, for he made whoever heard him feel happier than they had felt before. But what was little Tommy Smith doing to show how grateful he was to the bird that gave him so much pleasure? Why, I am sorry to say that he was trying to find the poor

THE HARE

lark's nest, so that he might take away the eggs which were in it,—those eggs which the mother lark had been taking so much trouble to keep warm, so that little baby larks might come out of them, which she meant to feed and take care of till they were grown up, and could fly and sing like herself. It was the thought of those eggs, and of the mother bird sitting upon them, which made the lark himself sing so gladly up in the air, for, when he looked down, he fancied he could see them; and he knew that there was someone waiting for him there who would be glad to see him again, when he came down to roost. But Tommy Smith did not think of this, for nobody had talked to him about it. All he thought of was how he could get the eggs, so that he could take them away with him, and show them to other boys.

Ah! what was that? How gracefully the cowslips waved, and up went a lark into the sky; and as he rose he seemed to shake a song out of his wings. Tommy Smith thought there was sure to be a nest close to where he had risen, so he went to look; but before he had got to the place, away went something—something brown like a lark, but ever so much larger, and, instead of flying, it galloped along over the ground; so, you see, it was not a bird at all. What was it? Tommy Smith knew well enough, for he had often seen such an animal before. "Ha!" he cried. "Puss! puss! A hare! a hare!" and he sent the stick which he had in his hand whizzing after it; but, I am glad to say, he did not hit it.

The hare did not seem so very frightened. Perhaps he knew that he could run away faster than any stick thrown by a little boy could come after him. At anyrate, before he had gone far, he stopped, and then he turned round, and raised himself right up, almost on his hind legs, and looked back at Tommy Smith.

"Well," he said, as Tommy Smith came up; "you see you cannot catch me."

"No," said Tommy Smith—he was getting quite accustomed to having talks with animals,—"you run too quickly."

"For my part," said the hare, "I wonder how any little boy who has a kind heart can like to tease and frighten a poor, timid

THE HARE

animal who is persecuted in so many ways as I am."

"What do you mean by 'persecuted'?" said Tommy Smith. "That is a word which I don't understand. It is too long for me."

"It is a great pity," the hare went on, "that a little boy should always be *doing* something which he does not know the word for. To 'persecute' people is to be very cruel to them, and whenever you hurt, or annoy, or frighten, or ill-treat any of us animals, then you are persecuting us."

"If I had known that," said Tommy Smith, "I would not have done it."

"Then you mustn't do it any more," said the hare; "and especially not to me, because I have so many enemies who are always trying to injure me."

"Why, what enemies have you?" said Tommy Smith.

"Plenty," the hare said. "First, there is that wicked animal the fox, who is always ready to kill and eat me whenever he has the chance. He is very cunning, and, as he knows he cannot run fast enough to catch me, he tries all sorts of ways to pounce upon me when I am not expecting it. Sometimes he will wait by a hole in the hedge that he has seen me go through, and when I come to it again, he springs out and seizes me with his teeth and kills me, for he is much stronger than I am. Then sometimes one fox will chase me past a place where another fox is hiding, and then the fox that was hiding jumps out at me, and they both eat me together."

"How wicked!" said Tommy Smith.

"Is it not?" said the hare. "And then there is that horrid little creature the weasel. He follows me about till he catches me, and then he bites me in the throat, so that I bleed to death."

"That *is* horrid of him," said Tommy Smith. "But there is one thing which I cannot understand. The weasel does not go so very fast, and you can run faster than a horse. I am sure that if you were to run away, he would never be able to catch you."

"You don't know what it is," said the hare. "That odious little animal follows me about, and never leaves off. You see, wherever I go I leave a smell behind me."

"Do you?" said Tommy Smith. "That

THE HARE

seems very funny. Why, I am close to you, and I don't smell anything."

"Little boys cannot smell nearly as well as animals," said the hare. "However, I don't *quite* understand it myself, for I am sure I am as clean as any animal can be, and there is nothing nasty about me; and yet whenever my feet touch the ground, they leave a smell upon it. That is my *scent*; but other animals have their scent too as well as I, so I needn't mind about it. Now the weasel has a very good nose, so that he is able to follow the scent that I have left on the ground, until he comes to where I am; and, besides, when I know that that cruel little animal is following me, I get so frightened that I cannot run away, as I would from you, or from a fox, or a dog. And so he comes up and kills me."

"Poor hare!" said Tommy Smith. "I feel very sorry for you. I am afraid that you are not clever like other animals, or else you would escape and get away more often. The rat would run down a hole, I am sure, and so would the rabbit. I have often seen him do it."

"Pray do not compare me to the rabbit,"

said the hare. "I have twice as much sense as he has, and I can tell you that you make a great mistake if you think I am not clever, for I am very clever indeed, as I will soon show you. If you will follow me a few steps, I will take you to the place where I was lying when you frightened me out of it. See, here it is. Look how nicely the grass is pressed downward and bent back on each side, so that it makes a pretty little bower for me to rest in when I am tired of running about. That is better, I think, than a mere hole in the ground; and, for my part, I look upon burrowing as a very foolish habit. *I* prefer fresh air, and I think that it is much nicer to see all about one than to live in the dark. This little bower of mine is what people call my *form*, and I am so fond of it that, however often I am driven away, I always come back to it again. And now, how do you think I get into this form of mine? I have told you that wherever I go I leave a scent upon the ground; so if I just came to my form and walked into it, any animal that crossed my scent would be able to follow it till he came to where I was. Now, what do you think I do to prevent this?"

"I don't know," said Tommy Smith, after he had thought a little; "I don't see how you can prevent it, for you must come to your form on your feet,—you cannot fly."

"No," said the hare; "but I can jump. Look!" And he gave several leaps into the air, which made Tommy Smith clap his hands and call out, "Bravo! how well you do it!"

"Now," said the hare, "when I am coming back to my form, I leap first to this side and then to that side, and then I make a very big jump indeed, and down I come in my own house. Of course, by doing this, I make it much more difficult for a fox or a weasel to smell where I have been, for it is only where my feet touch the ground that I leave my scent upon it."

"Ah, I see," cried Tommy Smith; "so, when you make long jumps, your feet will not touch the ground at so many places as they would if you only just ran along it."

"Of course not," said the hare.

"And then there will not be so many

places for a dog or a fox to smell where you have been," said Tommy Smith.

"Not nearly so many," said the hare; "that is the reason why I do it. I hope you think *that* quite as clever as just running down a hole, which is what the rat and the rabbit do."

"I think it very clever, indeed," said Tommy Smith; "and I see now that you are a clever animal."

"I have other ways of escaping when I am chased," the hare went on; "and I think, when you have heard them, you will confess they are quite as clever as anything which that conceited animal, the rat, has shown you. As to the rabbit, I say nothing. He is a relation of mine, and we have always been friendly. But the brains are not on *his* side of the family."

"Please go on, Mr. Hare," said Tommy Smith. "I should like to hear all you can tell me."

"Well," the hare said, "I have told you about the fox and the weasel, but they are not my only enemies. I have others—horses and dogs, and, worst of all, hard-hearted men and women, who ride the horses, and teach the dogs to run after me,

and to catch me. It is a pretty sight to see them all meet together in some field or lane. First one rides up, and then another, until there are quite a number. They laugh and talk whilst they wait for the huntsman to come with his pack of hounds. All are merry and light-hearted; even the horses neigh, they are in such spirits. Does it not seem funny that one creature's wretchedness should make so many creatures happy? And there are women—ladies, some of them quite young, and *so* pretty—like angels. I have seen them smile as if they could not hurt any living thing. You would have thought that they had come to stroke me, instead of to hunt me to death. But I know better. They are not to be trusted. They have soft cheeks, and soft eyes, and soft looks, but their hearts are hard.

"At last, up comes the huntsman, in his green coat and black velvet cap. He cracks his whip, and the dogs leap and bark around him—*such* a noise! I hear it all as I lie crouched in my form, and my heart beats with terror. But I cannot lie there long, for now they are coming towards me. I start up, and run for my life. Away I go, one poor, timid animal, who never hurt anyone, and after me come men and women, boys and girls, horses and dogs, all happy, and all thinking it the finest thing in the world to hunt and to kill—a hare."

"Are the dogs greyhounds?" said Tommy Smith.

"No," answered the hare; "the dogs I am talking about now are not greyhounds, but beagles. They hunt me by scent, but the greyhound hunts me by sight, for he runs so fast that he can always see me."

"Does he run as fast as you do?" asked Tommy Smith.

"Yes, indeed," said the hare; "he runs much faster, but he does not always catch me, for all that. When he is close behind me, I stop all of a sudden, and crouch flat on the ground. The greyhound cannot stop himself so quickly, for he is not so clever as I am. He runs right over me, and it is several seconds before he can turn round again. But *I* turn round as soon as he has passed me, and then I run as fast as I can the other way, so that, when he starts after me again, he is a good way behind, When he catches up to me, I do the same thing again. This clever trick of mine is called *doubling*, and I *am* so proud of it, for if it was not for that, the greyhound would catch me directly."

"Then does he never catch you?" said Tommy Smith.

"He never has yet," said the hare. "But I have other ways of getting away from him, as well as from other dogs, and I will tell you some of them. Sometimes I run under a gate. The dogs are too big to do this, so they are obliged to jump over it. Then, when they are near me, on the other side I double, in the way I told you, run as fast as I can back to the gate, and go under it again. Of course they have to jump over it a second time, and in this way I keep running under the gate and making them jump over it until they are quite tired, for, of course, it is more tiring to jump over anything than only to run under it. At last, when they are too tired to run any more, I slip quietly through a hedge and gallop away."

"Bravo!" cried Tommy Smith.

The hare looked very pleased, and said, "I see that you are not at all a stupid boy, so I will tell you something else. Now, supposing you were being chased across the fields by a lot of dogs, and you were to come to a flock of sheep, what would you do?"

Tommy Smith thought a little, and then he said, "I think I should call out to the shepherd and ask him to help me."

"Yes, and I daresay he *would* help *you*," said the hare, "for he would remember the time when *he* was a little boy, and he would feel sorry for you. But he would not feel sorry for *me*, who am only a little hare (he was never *that*, you know). He would throw his stick at me, as you did, and then he would do all he could to help the dogs to catch me. No, it is not the shepherd that I should ask to help me, but the sheep—*they* are so gentle,—and when I came to them I should run right into the middle of them, and then the dogs would not be able to find me."

"But would not the dogs follow you in amongst the sheep and catch you there?" said Tommy Smith.

"No," said the hare, "they would not be able to; for the flock would keep together, so that the dogs could only run round the outside of it. But *I* should keep right in the middle, and wherever the sheep went, I should go with them; *I* could run between their feet, you know. Besides, the dogs would not be able to see me amongst so many sheep."

" No," said Tommy Smith. "But could not they still follow you by your scent?"

"No, indeed, they could not," said the hare; "for, you see, sheep have a stronger scent than I have, and they would put down their feet just in the very place where I had put down mine, and then their scent would hide mine. So, you see, by hiding amongst a flock of sheep I should save my life, for the dogs would not be able either to see me, or smell me, or to follow me, even if they could."

"Have you ever done it?" said Tommy Smith.

"Oh yes!" said the hare; "and there is something else which I have done. Sometimes when the dogs were chasing me, I have run to where I knew another hare was sitting, and I have pushed that hare out of his place, so that the dogs have followed *him* instead of *me*. *I* sat down where *he* had been sitting, and they all went by without finding it out."

"Well," said Tommy Smith, "that may have been very clever, but I don't think it was at all kind to the other hare."

The hare looked a little surprised at this, as if he had not thought of it before. "One hare should help another, you know," he said; "and, besides, I daresay the dogs did not catch him after all. *He* may have found *another* hare."

Tommy Smith was just beginning with "Oh, but"—when the hare said, "Never mind!" rather impatiently, and then he continued, "And now I am going to tell you something which will show you that, although I am not a large or a fierce animal, I can sometimes be revenged on those who injure me, though they are larger and fiercer than myself."

"Oh, do tell me," said Tommy Smith, for the hare had paused a little, and seemed to be thinking.

"Ah!" he began again; "how well I remember it. I was very nearly caught that time. How fast the greyhounds ran, and how close behind me they were! What could I do to get away? I had gone up steep hills to tire them; and I *had* tired them, but then I had tired myself still more. I had run up one side of a hedge and down the other, so that they should not see me, and then I had gone through the roughest and thorniest part of that hedge, in hopes that they would not be able to follow. But they had kept close after me all the time, and now they were just at my heels. Then I doubled. Oh, how close I lay on the ground as the greyhounds leaped over me! I saw their white teeth, and their glaring eyes, and their red tongues lolling out of their great open mouths. But they had missed me, and I was saved for a little while. But where was I to run to next? There were no hedges now; no woods, or hills, or rocky ground, nothing but smooth level grass, which is just what greyhounds love to race over. Was there no escape? Yes. What was that long line far away where the green grass ended and the blue sky began? White birds were wheeling above it, and, from beneath, came a sound as though a giant were whispering. That was the sound of the sea, and the long line meeting the sky was the line of the cliffs. Oh, if I could reach it! But, first, I had to double — once — twice — three times;

over me they flew, and off I darted again. And now the line grew nearer, the white birds looked larger as they sailed in the air, and the whispering sound was changing to a moan—to a roar. Yes, I was close to it now, but the greyhounds were just behind me, and their hot breath blew upon my fur. They had caught me! No. On the very edge of the cliffs I doubled once more, and *once* more they went over me."

"And over the cliffs?" said Tommy Smith.

"Yes," said the hare; "over me, and over the cliffs as well. Something hid the sky for a moment,—a dark cloud passed above me. Then the sky was clear again; and there were no greyhounds now. Over and over, down, down, down they went, and were dashed to pieces on the black rocks, and drowned in the white waves. I know they were, for I peeped over the edge and saw it. You may ask the sea-gulls, if you like. They saw it too."

"Were they all drowned?" said Tommy Smith.

"Yes, all," said the hare.

"And were you glad?" he asked, for it seemed to him very dreadful.

THE HARE

"Well," the hare said, "I was glad to escape, of course, and so would you have been. But yet I could not help feeling sorry for the poor dogs, because they had been *taught* to chase me, and it was not their fault. Do you know who I should have liked to see fall over the cliffs instead of them?"

"Who?" said Tommy Smith.

"The cruel, hard-hearted men who taught them," said the hare. "It is they who ought to have been drowned, and I am very sorry that they were not."

"You poor hare!" said Tommy Smith, as he stroked its soft fur, and played with its long, pretty ears. "It is very hard that you should always be hunted, and I do think that you are very badly treated. But what clever ways you have of escaping! Do you know, I think you are the cleverest animal I have had a talk with yet, and I like you very much."

"Ah! it is all very well to say that now," said the hare. "But who was it that threw a stick at me?"

"I never will again," said Tommy Smith. "You know you jumped up all of a sudden, so that I had no time to think.

But I did not come out on purpose to throw it at you. I only wanted to find a lark's nest, so as to get the eggs."

When the hare heard that, I cannot tell you how sad and grieved he looked. "What!" he said. "Would you take the poor lark's eggs away, and make it unhappy? No, no; if you really like me, as you say you do, you must promise me not to do anything so cruel as that. The lark is the best friend I have. He sings to me as I lie in my form, and consoles me for all my troubles. His voice cheers me too, when I am being chased by the dogs, for he always seems to be saying, 'You will get away; I know you will get away.' Then sometimes he comes down to roost quite close to me, and we talk to each other. *He* tells *me* what it is like up above the clouds, and *I* tell *him* all that has been going on down here. He has *his* trials too, for there are hawks that try to catch *him*, just as there are greyhounds that try to catch *me*; so we sit and comfort each other. Promise me never to be unkind to my friend the lark."

"I won't hurt him," said Tommy Smith. "And if ever I find his nest with eggs in

THE HARE

it, I will only just look at them and leave them there."

"Oh, thank you," the hare said; "and you won't hurt me either?"

"No, indeed, I won't," said Tommy Smith. "Do you know, I begin to think that it would be better not to hurt any animal."

"Oh, much better!" said the hare, as he skipped gladly away. "Except the fox,—and the weasel, you may hurt *him*—if you can catch him." He said that, of course, because he *was* a hare, and felt prejudiced. You must not think *I* agree with him. Only a critic or a silly person would think *that*.

CHAPTER VI.

THE GRASS-SNAKE AND ADDER

*"Tommy Smith has a talk with the grass-snake, and then
With the adder: they're both as conceited as men."*

WHEN Tommy Smith had said good-bye to the hare, he thought he would walk home through some woods which were not far off. So off he set towards them, and as he went along he said to himself, "I know there are a great many animals that live in the woods. Now I wonder which of them will be the first to have a talk with me. Let me see. The pigeon and the squirrel both live there, for I have often seen them together on the same tree. And then there is the —" Good gracious! What was that just gliding out from under a bush? Tommy Smith gave a start and a jump, and well he might, for it was a large snake, perhaps three feet long. He was so surprised that, at first, he didn't quite know what to do, and before he had made up his mind, it was too late to do any-

THE GRASS-SNAKE AND ADDER 75

thing, for the snake had wriggled away into another bush. "It was an adder," said Tommy Smith out loud. "That, at least, is an animal which I *ought* to kill, because it is poisonous."

"I beg your pardon," said a sharp, hissing voice. "I am not an adder, and I am *not* poisonous."

Tommy Smith looked all about, but he could see nothing. Still, he felt sure that it must be the snake who had spoken, because the voice came from the very centre of the bush into which he had seen it go. So he answered, "Of course it is very easy for you to say that, but everybody knows that snakes are poisonous, and, if you are not a snake, I should just like to know what you are."

"I did not say that I was not a *snake*," said the voice again. "Of course I am, but I am not an adder for all that. There are two different kinds of snakes in this country. One is the adder, which is poisonous, and the other is the grass-snake, which is quite harmless. Now *I* am the grass-snake, so if you had killed me, you would have done something very wrong, for you would have killed a poor harmless animal."

"Well," said Tommy Smith, "if that is true, I am glad I didn't kill you. But are you quite sure?"

"If you don't believe *me*," said the snake, "you must get some good book of natural history, and there you will find it mentioned that we grass-snakes are quite harmless. It is the great superiority which our family have always had over that of the adder. People may call *him* a 'poisonous reptile,' but they cannot speak of *us* in that way. If they were to, they would only show their ignorance."

"But how am I to know which is one and which is the other?" asked Tommy Smith.

"You will not find *that* very difficult," the grass-snake answered; "and if you will promise not to hurt me, I will come out from where I am and show you."

Of course Tommy Smith promised (you see he was getting a much better boy to animals than he used to be), and directly he had, the snake came gliding out from under the bush, and lay on the ground

THE GRASS-SNAKE AND ADDER 77

just at his feet. "Now," he said, "to begin with, I am a good deal longer than an adder. I should just like to see the adder that was three feet long, and *I* am an inch longer than that. No, indeed! Whenever you see such a fine, long snake as I am, you may be sure that it is a nice grass-snake, and not a nasty adder."

"I won't forget that," said Tommy Smith. "But, I suppose, snakes grow like other animals. How should I be able to tell you from an adder if I were to meet you before you were three feet long?"

"Why, by my skin, to be sure!" said the grass-snake. "Look how beautifully it is marked, and what a fine greenish colour it is. I may well be proud of it, for a very great poet indeed has called it 'enamelled,' and says that it is fit for a fairy to wrap herself up in. Think of *that*! The adder's is quite different, only a dull, dirty brown, which I *might* call ugly if I were ill-natured. But I am *not*, so I will only say that it is plain. I don't think any fairy would like to wrap herself in *his* skin."

"But are there fairies?" said Tommy Smith.

"There are, as long as you are a little boy," said the grass-snake; "but as soon as you are grown up there will be none."

"How funny!" said Tommy Smith. "But do you know, Mr. Grass-Snake, I should not like to wrap myself up in your skin, even if I could, because it is so hard and covered with scales. And besides, how could the fairies get into it without killing you first? I don't suppose you can change it as the frog and the toad do."

"Not change it!" said the grass-snake. "And why not, pray? I should think myself a very stupid animal if I could not do *that*. Of course I change it, and then it looks and feels quite different to what it did when it was on me. You see, it is only just the outer part which comes off. That is quite thin, and I don't think you would find it *very* much harder than the petal of a flower. Some day, perhaps, you may find it if you look about in the grass or the bushes; for I rub myself against the grass or bushes to get it off."

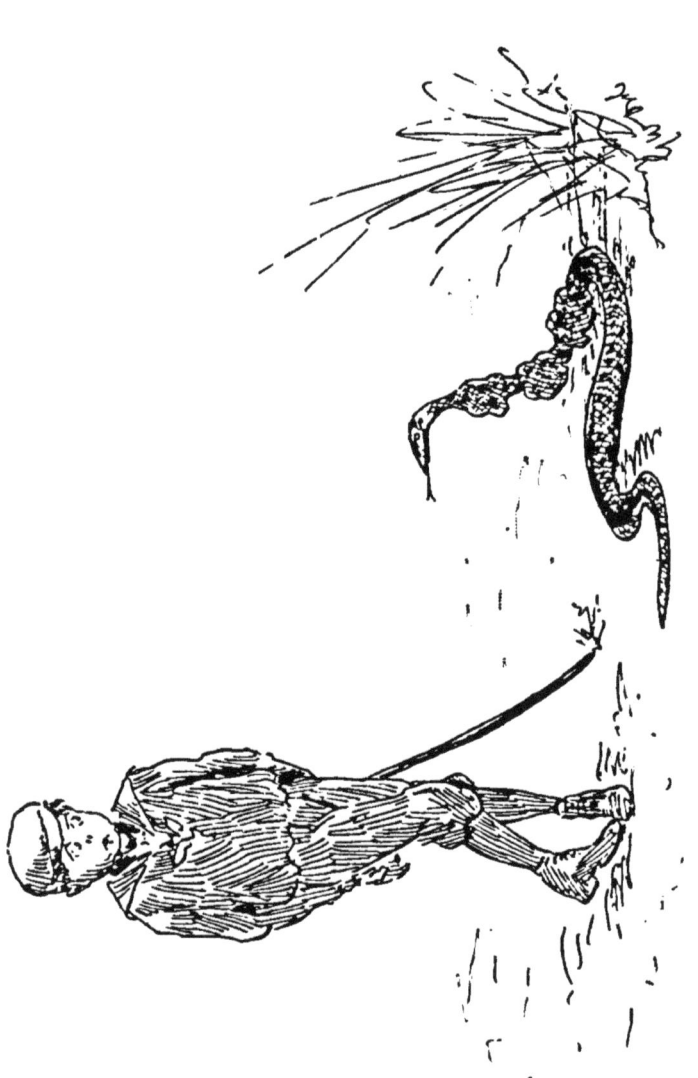

"THERE ARE THREE FROGS IN MY STOMACH AT THE MOMENT"

THE GRASS-SNAKE AND ADDER 79

"Then you do not swallow your skin as the toad does?" Tommy Smith asked.

"I should not like to do anything so nasty," said the grass-snake angrily, "and I wish you wouldn't keep talking to me about frogs and toads. They are very low animals, and only fit to be eaten."

Tommy Smith was quite shocked when he heard this, and he said, "Take care, Mr. Grass-Snake. Frogs and toads are very useful animals, and my friends, too. So I won't let you eat them."

"That is talking nonsense," said the grass-snake. "You can't help my eating them, especially frogs. Why, there are three frogs in my stomach at this moment."

Directly Tommy Smith heard that, he made a dart at the grass-snake, and caught hold of him before he could get away. I don't know what he meant to do. Perhaps he meant to kill the poor snake, which would have been very wrong, as you will see. But before he had time to do anything at all, two curious things happened. One was that the snake opened his mouth very wide indeed, and out of it came first one, then another, and then a third frog. Yes; three large frogs came out of the snake's mouth, one after the other, and there they all lay on the grass. That was one funny thing, and the other was that, as soon as Tommy Smith caught hold of the snake, the snake began to smell in a way that was not at all pleasant. Indeed, it was such a *very* nasty smell that Tommy Smith was glad to drop him, so that he got away into the bush again.

"Ah, ha!" the snake said, as soon as he was safe, "I thought you wouldn't hold me very long. Just look at your hand now."

Tommy Smith looked at his hand. It had a thick yellowish fluid on it, which made it feel quite moist, and it was this fluid which had such a disagreeable smell. He was very much offended with the grass-snake, and he called out to him, "I think that is a very nasty trick to play, indeed."

"I thought you wouldn't like it," replied the grass-snake, "and that is just why I did it. I wanted you to let me go, and, you see, you very soon had to. I always do that when anyone catches me; and, for my part, I think it is a very clever idea of mine."

"But how do you do it?" asked Tommy Smith, whilst he stooped down and wiped his hand on the grass.

"Why, I hardly know," said the grass-snake. "It comes naturally to me. Nobody can be cleaner or more well-behaved than I am, as long as I am treated properly. But when I am attacked, and my life is in danger, I do the only thing which I can do to protect myself. It is just as if you had a bottle of something which smelt so strongly that when you took out the cork and sprinkled it about, nobody could stay in the room. Now I have something which smells like that, only instead of keeping it in a bottle, I carry it under my skin, and when I want to use it, then, instead of taking out a cork, I just open my skin, and it comes out in little drops all over me."

"Open your skin?" said Tommy Smith. "Why, how do you do that?"

"I don't know *how* I do it," said the grass-snake, "but I *do* do it."

"Well," Tommy Smith said, "however you do it, I think it is a very nasty habit.

And besides, I shouldn't have caught hold of you if you hadn't told me that you had been eating frogs. I think it is very cruel of you to eat them. Why do you do it?"

"Why do I do it?" answered the grass-snake. "Why, because I feel hungry, to be sure. Why do you eat sheep, and oxen, and pigs, and ducks, and fowls, and turkeys?"

"Oh! but everybody eats them," said Tommy Smith.

"Every *snake* eats frogs," said the grass-snake. "We were made to eat them, and the frogs were made for us to eat. That is my theory. It is a good one, I feel sure, for it explains *the facts* and makes *me* feel comfortable."

"But they are so useful," said Tommy Smith; "and they do so much good in the garden."

"I don't eat them all," said the grass-snake, "and I don't often go into gardens. Frogs and toads may be very useful, but perhaps if I didn't eat some of them there would be too many of them in the world, and then, instead of being useful, they would be a nuisance. You see, I don't eat them all. I leave just as many as are

THE GRASS-SNAKE AND ADDER 83

wanted, as long as *you* don't kill them. But if *you* were to kill them too, then there would be too few."

Tommy Smith thought a little, and then he said, "Are you obliged to eat them?"

"Of course I am," said the grass-snake, "just as much as you are obliged to eat beef and mutton. You would think it very hard if you were to be killed just for eating your dinner. Then why should you want to kill me for eating mine? No, no; take my advice, and learn this lesson. Never kill one animal for eating another animal."

Tommy Smith thought over this for a little, and it seemed to him to be right "After all," he thought, "the frog and the toad eat insects, and if no animal might eat any other animal, then a great many animals would die of starvation, and that would be very dreadful." So he said to the grass-snake, "Well, Mr. Grass-Snake, I think you are right, and, if you come out of your bush, I will not try to catch you any more." So the grass-snake came wriggling out again, and then Tommy Smith asked him why he had brought the frogs out of his mouth after he had eaten them.

"It was because you frightened me," said the grass-snake. "You see, I wanted to get away, and, with three frogs inside me, I felt rather heavy. But as soon as the frogs were gone I was much lighter, and could go much quicker. Now don't you think it was a *very* clever idea?"

"I don't think it was a very *clean* idea," said Tommy Smith; "but as you were frightened, perhaps you couldn't help it. But now, Mr. Grass-Snake, are there any other clever things which you can do, and which are not quite so nasty? If there are, I should like to hear about them."

"I can lay eggs," said the grass-snake, "which is more than the adder can do."

"But can you really lay them?" said Tommy Smith; "and do you make a nest for them, like a bird?"

"No," said the grass-snake. "A bird makes a nest for her eggs because she has to sit on them, and she wants a nice, comfortable place to sit in. Now I don't sit on my eggs, for that is not at all necessary. I just find a nice, warm, moist place for them, and when I have laid them there, I go away and leave them. I have no time

THE GRASS-SNAKE AND ADDER 85

to sit on them like a bird. I am much too busy."

"But how are your eggs ever hatched?" said Tommy Smith.

"Oh," said the grass-snake, "I am so clever that I know the heat of the place where they lie will be enough to hatch them. So when they are once safely laid, I don't bother about them any more."

"Yes," said Tommy Smith; "but if you go away, who is there to look after the young snakes when they come out of the egg?"

"They look after themselves," said the grass-snake. "Birds are like little boys and girls. They are great babies, and want someone to take care of them whilst they are young. But we snakes are so clever that as soon as we come into the world we can take care of ourselves, and don't want anyone to help us."

"I should like to see some of your eggs," said Tommy Smith. "What are they like?"

"They are white," said the grass-snake, "and they are joined together in a long string, sometimes as many as sixteen or even twenty. So you may think how beautiful they look, like a necklace of very large pearls. Only they are not hard like pearls. Their shell is soft, and not at all like the shell of a bird's egg."

"I *should* like to see them," said Tommy Smith.

"Well," said the grass-snake, "you must look about in manure-heaps, and then, perhaps, you will find some. That is the sort of place that I like to lay them in."

Tommy Smith thought that this was another nasty habit of the grass-snake, but he didn't like to say so, because he had said it twice before; so, after a little while, he said, "And do you really like being a snake, Mr. Grass-Snake?" You see he had to say something, and he didn't quite know what to say.

"Like it?" said the grass-snake. "Of course I do. I should be very sorry to be anything else. Yes, we snakes have a happy life. In summer we crawl about and eat frogs, and in winter we find some nice place to go to sleep in."

"Then do you sleep all the winter?" said Tommy Smith.

"Of course," said the grass-snake. "What else is there to do? There are no frogs in winter, and it is cold and unpleasant. The

THE GRASS-SNAKE AND ADDER 87

best thing is to go to sleep, and that is what I always do."

Now whilst Tommy Smith was talking to the grass-snake he kept looking at the poor dead frogs that were lying on the grass, and you can think how surprised he was when, all at once, one of them moved a little, and then began to crawl away very slowly. Then the others moved, and began to crawl away too. So they were not dead after all. You see, when a snake eats a frog (or anything else), he does not chew it, as we do, but just swallows it whole, and then sometimes the frog will keep alive for some time inside the snake's stomach. Tommy Smith spoke to the frogs, but they were too faint to answer. So he took them up, and washed them in a little ditch which was close by, and then laid them in a nice long tuft of grass. When he had done that, he came back to where he had left the grass-snake, but he did not find him there again. "Where are you?" he called out. "Do you mean me?" said a voice quite near him. It was a hissing voice, certainly, and sounded a good deal like the grass-snake's. But still it did not sound quite the same, Tommy Smith thought. So he said, "I mean you, if you are the grass-snake," in rather a doubtful tone of voice. "No, indeed," hissed the voice again, "I am something better than a grass-snake. *I* am an adder." And as the adder said this, he came crawling out from a little clump of furze-bush, where he had lain hidden.

Tommy Smith saw that what the grass-snake had said was true, for the adder's body was shorter and of a duller colour than the grass-snake's. His head, too, was different. It was flatter, and swelled out more on each side where it joined the neck, so that the neck looked smaller in proportion to the size of the head. Altogether, Tommy Smith felt sure that the next time he went out for a walk and saw a snake, he would be able to tell whether it was a grass-snake or an adder. "And if it is an adder," he said to himself, "why, I ought to kill it." And then he said out loud, "Mr. Adder, you don't seem at all afraid of me; but, do you know, I think I ought to kill you, because you are poisonous."

"*I* think you ought to leave me alone because I am poisonous," said the adder.

THE GRASS-SNAKE AND ADDER

"For if you were to try to kill me, I should have to bite you, and then, perhaps, *I* should kill *you*."

Tommy Smith did not like this remark of the adder's at all. He began to feel afraid himself, and he would have liked to have run away. But he thought that if he did, the adder might attack him when his back was turned. So he stood quite still, and only said, "Why aren't you harmless like the grass-snake?"

"That is not a very polite question!" said the adder in reply. "*I* belong to the poisonous branch of the family, and I am proud to belong to it. The grass-snake is a poor creature, and I pity him. I should like to see anyone catch *me* in the same way that they catch *him*. I would soon teach them the difference between us."

"But you do so much harm," said Tommy Smith.

"What harm have I ever done *you*?" said the adder.

"You have not done me any harm," said Tommy Smith, "but that is because I have never seen you before now."

"*You* may never have seen *me*," said the adder, "but *I* have seen *you* very often.

Sometimes I have been quite near to where you were walking, but when I have heard you coming, I have just crawled out of the way, and let you go by without hurting you. Now don't you think that was very good of me? I should just like to know what you have to complain of."

"You have never hurt me, I know," said Tommy Smith. "But think how many people you do hurt."

"Do you know anybody that I have hurt?" asked the adder.

"No," answered Tommy Smith, "I don't know anybody; but I am sure you must have hurt a great many people, because you are poisonous."

"Well," said the adder, "I think you might walk about a long while asking people before you found anyone that I had done any harm to. I never interfere with people unless they interfere with me, so I think the best thing they can do is just to let me alone. It is true that my two front teeth are poisonous, and that I can kill some creatures by biting them. But these creatures are not men or women, but only mice or small birds or frogs. You know I have to eat them, so I may just as well kill

THE GRASS-SNAKE AND ADDER 91

them before I begin. The grass-snake eats *his* frogs alive. That is much more cruel than if he killed them first, as I do."

"How do you kill them?" said Tommy Smith. "I suppose you sting them with your forked tongue, and then they die."

"Did you not hear me say that I bit them," said the adder; "and that I had two poisonous teeth? My tongue is not poisonous at all. There is no more harm in it than there is in yours."

"Oh! but, Mr. Adder," cried Tommy Smith, "do you know I once went to the Zoological Gardens in London, and I saw the snakes there, and whenever one of them put out his tongue, as you do yours, the people all said, 'Look at its sting! Look at its sting!'"

"That is only because they were ignorant people," said the adder, "and did not know any better. No; it is the two long teeth in my upper jaw that are poisonous, and, if you will just kneel down, I will open my mouth so that you can see them, and then I can explain all about it to you."

Tommy Smith didn't quite like the idea of kneeling down and putting his face close to the mouth of the adder. He had heard of men who put their heads inside a lion's mouth, and he thought that this would be almost as dangerous. However, the adder promised not to bite him, and as he said he never *had* bitten a little boy in the whole of his life, and should not think of doing so without a proper reason, he thought he might trust him. So he knelt down and looked. Then the adder opened his mouth, and, as he did so, two little white things like fish-bones seemed to shoot forward into the front part of it. "Those are my two poison-fangs," he said. "When my mouth is shut, they lie back against my upper jaw, but as soon as I open it to bite anyone, they shoot forward so as to be in the right place." Tommy Smith looked at the teeth. They were as sharp as needles and almost as thin, but they were not straight like common needles, but curved backwards like crochet-needles. "What curious teeth!" he said.

"Perhaps they are more curious than you think," said the adder; "just look at the tips of them, and see if you notice anything."

Tommy Smith looked as the adder told

THE GRASS-SNAKE AND ADDER 93

him, and he was surprised to see a tiny little hole at the tip of each tooth. "Why, Mr. Adder," he said, "it seems to me as if your teeth were hollow and wanted stopping."

"They *are* hollow," said the adder, "and I will tell you why. At the root of each of them I have a little bag which is full of poison. You cannot see it, of course, because it is hidden under the flesh of my upper jaw. But things which cannot be seen are very often felt. Now, when I bite an animal, these little bags open, and a drop or two of poison runs down each tooth where it is hollow, so that it goes into the flesh of that animal and mixes with its blood."

"And does that kill it?" asked Tommy Smith.

"Oh yes!" answered the adder; "because I only bite small animals. It would not kill a horse, or a cow, or even a pig, unless it was very young. But it kills field-mice, and shrew-mice, and things of that sort."

"But there is one thing, Mr. Adder, which I don't understand," said Tommy Smith. "I thought that one had to swallow poison for it to kill one. But you say that this poison of yours goes into the blood."

"I don't know anything about poisons that have to be swallowed," said the adder; "I only know about *my* poison, and I use that in the way I have told you. *My* poison must go into the blood. If you were only to swallow it, I daresay it would not hurt you at all."

"I should not like to try," Tommy Smith said. "But are you going?" for the adder had begun to crawl away.

"Yes," said the adder; "I am going now, for I have plenty to do. I should not have wasted my time like this, only I heard that poor creature, the grass-snake, talking about himself, so I thought I would just show you what a much more important animal I am than he."

"I think that you are rather conceited, Mr. Adder," said Tommy Smith. "The grass-snake is very clever. He can lay eggs, and he says that is more than you can do."

"*I* should be ashamed to do such a thing," said the adder. "A young grass-snake *requires* an egg, but a young adder knows how to do without one. *We* can crawl as soon as we come into the world. As for my being conceited, perhaps I am, just a little. But that is natural. I can *never* forget that I have *poison* flowing in my veins. Now I will say good-bye, for I have plenty to do, and must not waste my time any longer."

"Good-bye, Mr. Adder," Tommy Smith called after him, for he thought he had better be friendly with such an animal. "I hope that you will never bite me." But the adder merely gave a contemptuous hiss, and was gone.

CHAPTER VII.

THE PEEWIT

*"To eat peewit's eggs to a peewit seems wrong,
So a hen MAY think hen's eggs to hens should belong."*

"PEE-WEE-EET! Pee-wee-eet!" That is what a bird kept saying as he flew in circles round Tommy Smith. Sometimes he flew quite a long way off, and sometimes he came so near him that it seemed as if he would settle on his head. "Pee-wee-eet! Pee-wee-eet!" And what a pretty bird this was! How his white breast glanced in the sun, and how the glossy green feathers of his back shone in it. He kept turning about in the air as he flew, so that Tommy Smith could see every part of him.

In fact, this bird was playing the strangest antics. Sometimes he would clap his wings together above his back, at least Tommy Smith thought he did; and then he would make such a swishing and whizzing with them, that really it was quite a loud noise—almost like a steam-

THE PEEWIT

engine. Then, all at once, he would turn sideways and make a dive down towards the ground, and sometimes (this was the funniest trick of all) he would tumble right over in the air, as if he had lost his balance and was really falling. If Tommy Smith had ever seen a tumbler pigeon it would have reminded him of one, but he never had. And all the while this bird kept on calling out, "Pee-wee-eet! pee-wee-eet!" as if he wanted Tommy Smith to speak to him, as, perhaps, he did.

"I know what bird *you* are," said Tommy Smith. "I have often seen you flying over the fields, but you have never come so close to me before. I think your name is"—

"Pee-wee-eet! pee-wee-eet! That is my name. They call me the peewit."

"Yes," said Tommy Smith; "because you say"—

"Pee-wee-eet! pee-wee-eet!" screamed the bird. "Yes, that is why. It is because I say 'Pee-wee-eet'"; and as the peewit said this, he made a sweep down and settled on the ground just in front of Tommy Smith. So close! Tommy Smith could almost have touched him with his hand. He *was* a handsome bird! *Now* he could see that, besides his beautiful green back and his white breast, he had a handsome black crest at the back of his head, that stuck out a long way behind it —as if his hair had been brushed up behind, Tommy Smith thought, only, of course, it was not hair, but feathers.

The peewit was not at all afraid, but looked up at Tommy Smith, with his head on one side, and said, "Yes, that is my name. A name isn't sensible if it hasn't a meaning. Some people call me the lapwing, but I don't know what *that* means. I would rather *you* called me the peewit. I like that name best. Well, now you may ask me some questions if you like." Tommy Smith would rather have listened to what the peewit had to tell him about himself first, and then asked him some questions afterwards, for, just then, he didn't quite know what questions to ask. But, of course, he had to say something, or it would have seemed rude, so he began with, "Please, Mr. Peewit, will you tell me why you say 'pee-weet' so often?"

"Why shouldn't I say it?" said the

THE PEEWIT

peewit. "It is my song, and I think it is a very good one too."

"But I don't call it a song at all," said Tommy Smith.

"*Don't* you?" said the peewit.

"No," said Tommy Smith. "It is not at all like what the lark or the nightingale sings. That is what *I* call singing."

"If all birds were to sing as well as each other," the peewit said, "perhaps you would not care to listen to any of them half so much. *Now* you say, 'How sweetly the lark sings,' or 'How beautifully the nightingale sings,' because they sing better than other birds. But if every bird was as clever at singing as they are, then to sing well would be such a common thing, that you would hardly notice it at all. As it is, you don't think about the lark nearly so much as the nightingale, because you hear him much oftener. So perhaps, after all, it is better that some birds should sing more sweetly than other birds. Don't you agree with me?"

"I don't know," said Tommy Smith. "I should never have thought of that, myself."

"There are a number of things that

little boys would never have thought of," said the peewit. "Besides," he went on, "however well a bird may sing, all he *means* by his singing is that he is very happy. That is what the lark means when he sings high up in the blue sky; and it is what the nightingale means when he sings all night long by his nest. And that is what I mean, too, when I sing, 'Pee-wee-eet! pee-wee-eet!' So if you look at it in that way, my song is just as good as theirs, or any other bird's."

Tommy Smith did not think the peewit was right in this opinion of his, but he thought that he had better not contradict him so early in the conversation. So he only said, "Then, I suppose, you must always be happy, Mr. Peewit, for you are always saying 'Pee-wee-eet'?"

"I am always happy as long as people don't shoot me, or take away my eggs," said the peewit. "Why should I not be? It is very pleasant to be alive."

"And the grass-snake said *he* was happy too," thought Tommy Smith. "Then, are *all* animals happy, Mr. Peewit?" he asked.

"Oh yes," the peewit answered, "they

all enjoy their life. That is why it is so wrong to kill them. For when you kill an animal, you take some of the happiness that was in the world out of it, and you can never put it back there again, however much you try."

"I never will kill animals any more," said Tommy Smith. "But now, Mr. Peewit, won't you tell me something about yourself? Do *you* do any clever things as well as the other animals that I have spoken to?"

"Why, haven't you seen the way I tumble about in the air?" said the peewit. "And don't you think that *that* is very clever? You couldn't do it yourself, however much you were to try."

"No," said Tommy Smith, "but then *I* have not got wings, you know. Perhaps if I *had* got wings, I would be able to do it as well as you."

"Do you think so?" said the peewit. "That is only because you are very conceited. Why, even the swallow can't do it. *He* is a splendid flier, and goes very fast. But, though you were to watch him for a whole day, you would not see him do such funny things in the air as I do.

As for the other birds—well, look at the cuckoo. What do you think of the way in which *he* flies? Why, he just goes along without doing anything at all. Do you think *he* could turn head over heels or make the noise with his wings that I do? If he can, then why doesn't he? I should just like to know that."

"Are you playing a game in the air when you fly like that, Mr. Peewit?" asked Tommy Smith.

"Yes," answered the peewit; "that is just what I am doing. Sometimes I play it by myself, but I like it better when there are some other peewits to play it with me. We do it to amuse ourselves, and because we are so happy and have such good spirits. But it is only in the springtime that we play such games, for we are happier then than at any other time of the year. In the autumn and winter we fly about in great flocks over the fields and marshes, or come down upon them and look for worms and slugs and caterpillars, for those are the things we eat. We are happy then, too, but not quite so happy as we are in the springtime, and you won't see us playing such pranks then, although there are a great many more of us together. Oh yes! it is a game, but it is a very useful kind of game, I can tell you."

"How is it useful?' asked Tommy Smith.

"Why, it prevents people from finding our eggs," answered the peewit. "I have told you that we only fly like this in the spring. Well, that is just the time when we lay our eggs. Now whilst the mother peewit is sitting quietly on her eggs, the father peewit keeps flying and tumbling about in the air. When you go for a walk over the fields, you do not notice the mother peewit on her eggs, for she sits quite still and never moves. But you can't help noticing the father peewit, and you only think of him. If you happen to go too near the place where the eggs are, the father peewit comes quite close to you, and flies round and round your head, as I did just now. You think that is very funny, and so you keep looking at him up in the air, and never think of looking on the ground where the eggs are."

"Are the eggs laid on the ground?" said Tommy Smith.

"Of course," said the peewit. "But let me go on. When the father peewit sees you are looking at him, he flies a little farther away from the eggs, and, of course, you follow him. Then he flies a little farther off still, and in this way he keeps leading you farther and farther away from the eggs, till he thinks they are safe, and then off he flies altogether."

"That is very clever," said Tommy Smith. "But supposing you didn't follow the father peewit, but kept walking towards where the eggs were, what would the mother peewit do?"

"Why, she would fly away before you got to her," said the peewit. "And you would find it very difficult to find the eggs even then."

"Then, is it only the father peewit that tumbles over in the air?" said Tommy Smith.

"It is he who does it most," said the peewit. "He has more time, and besides it would not be thought right for a mother peewit to throw herself about in that way whilst she has a family to attend to. When the mother peewit goes up from her eggs, she flies

THE PEEWIT

quietly away till she is a long way off. Then she settles somewhere on the ground, and waits for you to go away, and when you have gone away, she comes back to her eggs again."

"Then I suppose *you* are a father peewit?" said Tommy Smith.

"Oh yes," the peewit answered. "You have seen how *I* can tumble. And besides, look how long my crest is. The crest of the mother peewit is not nearly so long."

"Where is the mother peewit?" asked Tommy Smith—for he thought he would like to see her too.

"She is not far off," the peewit answered, "and she is sitting on her eggs."

"Oh! I should so like to see them," cried Tommy Smith. "May I?"

"If I show you them," said the peewit, "will you promise not to take them away."

"Oh yes, I promise not to," said Tommy Smith. "I will only look at them—unless you would be so kind as to give me one," he added.

"*Give* you one!" cried the peewit. "I would rather give you the bright green feathers from my back, or the beautiful crest that is on my head. Give you one, indeed! No, no; they are not things to be given away. But come along. You have promised that you will not take them, and I know you will not break your word." Then the peewit spread his wings, and rose into the air again, and began to fly along in front of Tommy Smith, who had to run to keep up with him. "Pee-wee-eet! pee-wee-eet!" he cried. "Come along. Come along."

"Oh, but you go so fast!" said Tommy Smith, panting. "I wish I had wings like you."

"I don't wonder at your wishing *that*," the peewit said. "*I* should think it dreadful if I could only walk and run." All at once the peewit flew down on to the ground again. "Here they are," he said, as Tommy Smith came up; "and what do you think? Why, one of them has hatched already; a day earlier than I expected."

"But where are the eggs?" asked Tommy Smith. "I don't see them, and I don't see any nest either. But what— Oh! there is the mother peewit sitting on the ground," he cried out suddenly.

And so she was, with her eggs underneath her. This time she did not fly away, for the father peewit had told her not to be uneasy.

"Oh, but there is no nest," said Tommy Smith. "She is sitting on the bare ground."

"*Bare*, indeed!" exclaimed the mother peewit. "There is plenty of sand on the ground, and what more can one want? Just look!" and as she spoke she moved a little to one side, and there, in a slight hollow, Tommy Smith saw four—no, three eggs, and something else, something that was soft and fluffy, so it could not be an egg, although it was the same size, and the same sort of colour, yellowish, with black spots. Why, could that be a little baby peewit? Yes, indeed it was, for it moved a little, and made a little chirping noise.

"Don't touch him," cried the father peewit. "He is too young for that."

"And little boys are so rough," said the mother peewit.

"But you may look at him," said the father peewit.

"Oh yes, do," said the mother peewit;

"and tell me what you think of him. Isn't he the prettiest little fluffy thing in the whole world?"

"Until the others are hatched," said the father peewit. "Then there will be three more, you know."

"To be sure there will," said the mother peewit, looking *very* proud; "and they will all be as pretty as each other. But I think this one will be the cleverest," she added. "There was a certain something in the way he chipped the shell, and he has lain in a thoughtful attitude ever since he came out."

"I am glad to hear it," said the father peewit. And then they both looked up at Tommy Smith, as if they expected him to say something.

But Tommy Smith was too busy to say anything just then. He had gone down on his hands and knees, and was looking at the eggs, for they interested him more even than the little peewit that had just been hatched. They were such funny-shaped eggs, large at one end and pointed at the other, something like a small pear, Tommy Smith thought, and they lay in the little hollow with

THE PEEWIT

their pointed ends all meeting together in the middle of it. They were of a greenish yellow colour, with great black splotches upon them. Of course they were much smaller than the eggs that a hen lays, but still, Tommy Smith thought, they were large eggs for a peewit to lay. A peewit is hardly so large as a pigeon, but these eggs were a good deal larger than a pigeon's egg. "Yes, they are very nice eggs," he said at last, as he got up from his hands and knees. "Are they good to eat?"

"Yes," said the father peewit, "they are"; and as he said this he looked *very, very* sad.

"Yes, they *are* good to eat," said the mother peewit, as she nestled down on her eggs again. "Oh, how I wish they were not!"

"Why?" said Tommy Smith. (He was only a little boy, or he would not have asked such questions.)

"I will tell you why," said the mother peewit. "There are bad men who come and take our eggs *because* they are so good to eat, and then they sell them to greedy wretches, who are still worse than themselves. Oh, how wicked men are! Just fancy! They eat our poor little children whilst they are still in their cradles."

"Yes," said the father peewit, "for the mere pleasure of eating, they will ruin thousands of families."

"Is it so *very* wicked to eat eggs?" asked Tommy Smith. "I have eaten a great many myself."

"What! peewit's eggs?" cried both the birds together.

"Oh no," said Tommy Smith feeling *very* uncomfortable. "But I have often eaten fowl's eggs."

"That is different," said the mother peewit. "We will say nothing about that."

"No, no," said the father peewit. "We do not wish to be censorious."

"What does that mean?" asked Tommy Smith, for it was a long word, and he did not remember having heard it before.

"I mean," said the father peewit, "that if people *only* ate fowl's eggs, peewit's eggs would be let alone, and that would be a very good thing. Fowls, you know, are accustomed to it, but we peewits have finer feelings."

"Yes," said the mother peewit; "we are more sensitive than common poultry."

Tommy Smith couldn't help remembering what the rat had said to him about asking the hen, and he thought he *would* ask her some day. But now he was talking to peewits. "You told me it was very difficult to find your eggs," he said.

"So it is," said the father peewit; "but it is not impossible."

"I wish it were," said the mother peewit. "But there are wicked men who learn how to do it, and then they can find them quite easily. Oh, what a wicked world it is!"

Tommy Smith didn't know what to say to comfort the poor peewits, until all at once an idea occurred to him. "Why do you lay eggs at all?" he said. "You know, if you didn't lay them, nobody could take them away from you."

"Not lay eggs?" cried the mother peewit. "Why, it is our duty to lay them. We have our duties to perform, of course."

"If we did *not* lay eggs," said the father

peewit (he looked *very* grave as he spoke), "there would soon be no more peewits in the world, and what do you suppose would happen then?"

Tommy Smith didn't know, so he said, "What *would* happen, Mr. Peewit?"

"It is too dreadful to think about," the peewit said. "The very idea of it makes one shudder. A world without peewits! Oh dear! a nice sort of world *that* would be!"

The mother peewit shook her head. "It could hardly go on, dear; could it?" she said.

"It *might*," answered the father peewit, "but there would be very little *meaning* in it."

Tommy Smith certainly thought the world might go on without peewits, but he didn't *quite* understand the last part of the sentence. "But it seems to me," he said to himself, "that *animals* think themselves very important." "And are *you* a useful animal?" he said aloud to the father peewit,—for the mother peewit was busy again with her eggs and the young one.

"Useful!" exclaimed the peewit. "Why,

THE PEEWIT

we are sometimes put into gardens to eat the slugs and the insects there. I suppose *that* is being useful."

"Oh yes," said Tommy Smith; "if you don't eat the cherries, or the strawberries, or the asparagus, or"—

"We are not vegetarians," said the peewit, "we prefer an animal diet, and we only eat things that do harm."

"But don't you eat worms?" said Tommy Smith.

"Of course we do," said the peewit.

"But I don't think worms do harm."

"If they don't, it is because we eat them," the peewit retorted. "If we didn't eat them, there would be too many of them, and then, of course, they would do harm."

"Well, when I grow up," said Tommy Smith, "I will have peewits in my garden as well as frogs, and—Oh! but do you agree with frogs?" he asked, for this was an important point.

"Young frogs agree very well with *us*," said the peewit. "So it comes to the same thing, doesn't it?"

"I don't know," said Tommy Smith. "Not if the old ones don't."

"As for the old ones," said the peewit,

"we leave them alone. They are too big to be interfered with. So, you see, that's all right too."

Tommy Smith didn't feel quite so sure about this. He couldn't help thinking that perhaps the peewits ate the little frogs. But, just as he was going to ask them this, he remembered that if he didn't make haste home, he would be late for dinner. Of course, as soon as he began to think about his own dinner, he forgot all about the peewit's, and said good-bye at once. So off he ran. The mother peewit just nodded to him as she sat on her eggs, but the father peewit rose up into the air again, and flew round him, and swished his wings, and tumbled about, and cried, "Pee-wee-eet! pee-wee-eet!" and Tommy Smith felt quite sure that he meant "Good-bye, good-bye."

CHAPTER VIII.

THE MOLE

*'If we're only contented, some cause we shall find
To be thankful: the mole thought it nice to be blind."*

THE next walk that Tommy Smith took was over some fields where there were a great many mole-hills. Of course, Tommy Smith had often seen mole-hills before, but I am not sure if he had ever seen a mole; for a mole, as you know, lives underneath the ground, and does not often come up to the top of it. So, when he saw a little black thing scrambling about in the grass, he cried out, "Oh! whatever is that?" and ran to it and picked it up.

"You won't *hurt* me, I know," said the mole (for it was one)—"and I don't mind your *looking* at me." You see Tommy Smith was getting a much better boy to animals, now that they had told him something about themselves, and the animals were beginning to find this out, and were not so frightened of him as they used to be.

Tommy Smith looked at the mole, and stroked it as it lay in his hand, and then he said, "Why, what a funny little black thing you are."

"Little!" said the mole; "I don't know what you mean by that. I am much bigger than the mouse or the shrew-mouse. You don't expect me to be as big as the rat, do you?"

"I don't know," said Tommy Smith, "but, you know, the rat is not so very big."

"He is as big as he requires to be, I suppose," said the mole, "and so am I. I have never felt too small in all my life, and I wonder that you should think me so. Why, look at those great hills of earth which I have flung up all over the fields. I am big enough to have made those, anyhow, and strong enough too. And look, how large and high they are."

"But are they so very high?" said Tommy Smith. "Why, I step over them quite easily."

"Dear me, that seems very wonderful," said the mole. "But I advise you not to do it often, for it must be a great exertion, and you might hurt yourself. But you must not think that because *you* are very big, *I* am very small. That would be very conceited."

Tommy Smith saw that he had not said the right thing, so he tried to think of something to say that the mole would like better. "Oh," he said at last, "what a very pretty, soft coat you have! I like it very much, indeed."

"Yes; feel it," said the mole. "It is a very handsome fur; and I can tell you something about it which is curious."

"What is that?" said Tommy Smith.

"Why, you may stroke it whichever way you like," answered the mole, "without hurting me. It is not every animal that has a coat like *that*. There is the cat, poor thing! If you stroke her fur one way, she is very pleased and begins to purr; but if you stroke it the other way, it hurts her, and she does not like it at all. That is because her hair is long and lies all one way. Now my hair is short, and it does not lie any way."

"I suppose you mean that it does not point either towards your head or your tail," said Tommy Smith.

"Yes, that is what I mean," said the mole. "Instead of that, it sticks straight up, and when you stroke it, it moves whichever way your hand moves, without making me feel at all uncomfortable."

"That is a very nice fur to have," said Tommy Smith. "Then, I suppose that sometimes if you were burrowing, and you wanted to go backwards for a little way, it would not hurt you to do so."

"Not at all," said the mole. "Now the poor cat could not do that. She could not go backwards in a burrow, because it would rub all her hair up the wrong way."

"But cats don't burrow," said Tommy Smith.

"Of course not," said the mole. "They know that they would not be able to, so they don't try. They are poor things."

Tommy Smith could not see why cats should be poor things because they didn't burrow, but the mole seemed quite sure of it, and he did not like to contradict him. "I suppose, Mr. Mole," he said, "that you are made for burrowing."

"Yes, I am," said the mole, "and I can do it better than any other animal in the world. You see, I have a pair of spades to help me, and I dig with both of them at the same time."

THE MOLE

"A pair of spades!" cried Tommy Smith in surprise. "Why, where are they? I don't see them."

"Where are they?" said the mole; "why, here they are, to be sure," and he stretched out his two little front feet, and moved them about.

"Ah, now I see what you mean," said Tommy Smith, and he bent down his head and began to look at them more closely.

The mole might well have called his feet spades, for they were shaped something like them, and he used them to dig with,—which is what spades are used for. They were short and broad, with five little toes, and each toe had a very strong claw at the end of it. These funny little feet stuck out on each side of the mole's body, and they were so very close to the body that they looked as if they had been sewn on to it. There did not seem to be any leg belonging to them at all. Of course there *were* legs, and very strong ones too, but they were so short, and so hidden under the skin, that Tommy Smith could not see them, although he felt them directly. The hind legs and feet were much smaller, and not nearly so strong, which, the mole said, was because they had not so much work to do. Between them there was a very short tail, just long enough, Tommy Smith thought, to take hold of and lift the mole up by. But he did not do this, in case he should be offended. "Well," said the mole, after Tommy Smith had looked at him for a little while, "what do you think of me? I hope you think me handsome."

"Yes, I think you are," Tommy Smith answered, though he did not feel quite sure of this. "At anyrate, your fur is handsome, for it is like velvet."

"Yes," said the mole; "and, do you know, I am sometimes called the little gentleman in the black velvet coat."

"It is not quite black," said Tommy Smith. "There is a greyish colour in it too. I think it would look very pretty if it was made into something. Oh, Mr. Mole," he cried all of a sudden, "now I remember that I have heard people talk about moleskin waistcoats!"

At this the mole gave a little squeak, and jumped quite out of Tommy Smith's hand, and then he began to burrow into the ground as fast as he could, and this was very fast indeed, so that before Tommy Smith had got over his surprise, he was almost out of sight. "Oh, Mr. Mole," he cried, "do come back!" but the mole was very angry, and would not consent to for some time.

"If I do," he said at last, "you must promise me never to talk in that way again."

"Oh, I never will," said Tommy Smith. "I quite forgot who I was talking to."

"Moleskin waistcoats, indeed!" said the mole. "I think the people who wear them are very wicked people. They never think how many poor little moles must be killed only to make one. I hope *you* have never worn a waistcoat like that?"

"Oh no," answered Tommy Smith, "I never have. Nobody has ever given me one."

"I hope you never will," said the mole; "for if you do, you will be almost as wicked a man as a mole-catcher, and he is the wickedest person I know of."

"A mole-catcher!" cried Tommy Smith; "then are there men who catch moles?"

"Oh yes, indeed there are," said the mole. "There are men who do that and nothing else."

"How do they do it?" asked Tommy Smith.

"They have traps," answered the mole, "which they put in the passages and corridors of our great underground palaces."

"Your houses, I suppose, you mean," said Tommy Smith.

"I mean what I say," said the mole. "You may live in a house, I daresay, but I think the place that I live in is quite large and fine enough to be called a palace, so I call it one."

"Oh! but it cannot be so big as the house that I live in," said Tommy Smith.

"Well," said the mole, "I should just like to know how long the longest corridor in your house is."

Tommy Smith thought to himself a little. The house he lived in was not a very large one, for his father was not a *very* rich man. There were not many passages in it, and he did not think the longest of them was long enough to be called a corridor. Still, he thought that they must be longer than the passages of a mole's house, and he couldn't help feeling rather proud as he said, "Oh! I don't know exactly, because I have never measured it, but perhaps it is six yards long."

"Six yards?" cried the mole. "Do you call *that* a corridor? Why, some of mine are more than twenty times as long as that. You might walk over a whole field without coming to the end of them. And how many corridors has your house got, then?"

"Oh, I think there are three," said Tommy Smith; but this time he didn't feel nearly so proud.

"Good gracious!" cried the mole. "Why, yours must be a very poor place to live in. I wish I could show you over my palace, but you are such an awkward size that you would never be able to get into it. My corridors are longer than yours, but they are not nearly so high. However, perhaps it is just as well that you can't get into it, for if you were once there, I am sure you would never want to go back again."

"Perhaps, Mr. Mole," said Tommy Smith, "as you can't show me over it, you will tell me what it is like."

"Well," said the mole, "I will; and

perhaps, if you are always a good boy, and *never* think of wearing a moleskin waistcoat, I will show it you some day from the outside; but that can only be when I have done with it, and am going to build a new one, for I should have to break open the roof for you to see into it. Well, then, the principal part of my palace is called the keep, or fortress,—*I* call it the fortress. It is very large, and the roof goes up into a beautiful, high dome. You know what a dome is, I suppose?"

"Oh yes," said Tommy Smith; for once he had been to London, and he remembered the dome of St. Paul's Cathedral.

"I wish you could see how high and stately it is," said the mole. "It goes right up into the bush ever so high."

"You mean 'into the air,' I think," said Tommy Smith.

"I mean what I say," said the mole; "into the bush. That is why you can't see it."

"Oh, but I can see it," said Tommy Smith. "I can always find your fortresses, Mr. Mole. I see lots of them every time I go out walking. They are not hidden at all. Why, there they are all over the field, and you know you told me to look at them yourself."

The mole gave a little choky laugh. "Oh dear!" he cried, "and do you *really* think that *those* are my fortresses? You are *very* much mistaken if you do. Why, they are only the hills that I throw up when I am making my tunnels and corridors. All you will find if you open them is a hole going down into one of those. Oh no; my fortress is not built there. It is carefully hidden under a bush or the root of a tree, so that you can't see it, however high it is. Only the wicked mole-catcher is able to find it, and I am very sorry he can."

This was a great surprise to Tommy Smith, for he had always thought that the mole lived under those little brown heaps of earth. But he had only thought so because he had never taken any trouble to find out about it. "I see you are cleverer than I thought, Mr. Mole," he said; "but I should like you to tell me something more about your palace and fortress."

"I told you that it was very large," said the mole, "and that it went up into a high dome outside. Inside, it is not nearly so high, but it is very nice and comfortable; and the floor and the sides and ceiling are always quite smooth and polished, for I polish them myself, and never leave it to the servants."

"But how do you polish them?" said Tommy Smith.

"Why, with my fur to be sure," said the mole. "I prefer that to a piece of wash-leather." (He laughed again as he said this, but Tommy Smith didn't know what for.) "My fur, as you see, is smooth too. If you were to walk down one of my corridors, you would be surprised to find how hard and smooth the sides of it are. That is because I am always running up and down them, and rubbing them with my fur."

"But doesn't that make you very dirty?" said Tommy Smith. "Surely the earth must get into your fur and stay there."

"It *never* stays there," said the mole with great pride. "I have a very strong muscle which runs all along my back just under the skin, and when I twitch that, every little piece of mould or earth that is in my fur flies out of it again. There' now I have twitched it. Look at me and see how clean I am, although I have only just come out of the ground. Oh no; there is never anything in *my* coat! It is a saying in our family that a mole *may* live in the dirt, but he is never *dirty*."

"That seems very funny," said Tommy Smith. "But tell me some more about the fortress that you live in."

"That is just what I was going to do," said the mole, "but you ask so many questions, that I am not able to get on. Now I will begin again, and perhaps it would be better if you were to say nothing till I have done."

So Tommy Smith sat down on the ground to listen, and the mole went on in these words:

"Inside my fortress there is a large room which is quite round. I call it my bedroom or dormitory, because sometimes I go to sleep there. There are two different ways of getting into it. One of them is by the floor, and that is easy. But the second way is by the ceiling, and that is much more difficult."

"By the floor and the ceiling?" cried Tommy Smith, quite forgetting what the mole had said. "How very funny! I get into *my* room through a door in one of the sides."

"Dear me!" said the mole. "Well, I should not like to enter a room in that way."

"Why not?" asked Tommy Smith.

"The idea of such a thing!" said the mole. "As for doors, they are things I don't understand. Galleries and tunnels are what I use, and I think them much grander."

"But"— Tommy Smith was beginning.

"Let me get on," said the mole. "I have two galleries inside my fortress, an upper one and a lower one. The lower one is the largest. It runs all round the ceiling of my bedroom. From it there are five little passages which run up into the upper one. That goes round in a circle too, but it is high up inside the dome of my fortress, and a long way above the ceiling of my bedroom. So what do you think I have done? I have made three little tunnels, which go from my upper gallery right into the top of my bedroom. I just run down one of them, and tumble into it through the ceiling."

"But can't you get into your bedroom from the lower gallery too?" asked Tommy Smith.

"Oh no," said the mole; "that would never do. It would be so easy; and a mole likes to do things that are difficult. I go into my lower gallery first, and then I go from that into my upper gallery. I can go by five different passages, and choose which I like.

"Five different passages! That is a lot," cried Tommy Smith.

"Yes; and there are three more from the upper gallery into the bedroom!" said the mole. "How many doors are there into *your* rooms?"

"Oh, one," said Tommy Smith.

"Only one!" said the mole. "That is very sad. Why, if I had only one tunnel into my room I should be almost ashamed to go through it. But then you have only a house to live in, and not a palace, as I have."

Tommy Smith thought that this was rather a grand way of talking, and he was just beginning, "Perhaps, if you were to see my house"—when the mole went on with, "Of course, such a fine palace as mine ought to have a good many fine roads leading up to it."

"Ought it?" said Tommy Smith; "and how many has it?"

"Seven," said the mole.

"Seven!" exclaimed Tommy Smith.

"Yes," said the mole, "and I make them all myself. Why, how many has yours?"

"It has only one," said Tommy Smith, "but I think that is quite enough."

"For a house, perhaps, it may be," said the mole; "but *I* should be sorry to have to put up with it. *My palace* has seven, and I know some very rich moles who have eight. These are the great corridors which some people call the high roads. Some of them run through fine avenues of tree-roots, and, you know, a fine avenue of tree-roots has a splendid appearance. They wind all about, and go for ever such a way, and there are smaller corridors which run out of them on each side, and spread all over the fields."

"You mean *under* the fields, Mr. Mole," said Tommy Smith; "for, you know, the grass grows over your corridors, and nobody can see them."

"I am very glad they can't," said the

THE MOLE

mole, "or my bedroom, or my nursery either."

"What, have you a nursery too?" said Tommy Smith. "Why, that is just as if you were a person."

"Of course I have a nursery," said the mole. "What should I do with my children if I had not? I could not have them always in the fortress, or playing about in the corridors. They would be quite out of place there, and very much in the way. So I have a nursery for them, and they lie there upon a nice warm bed, which I make myself, of young grass and other soft things."

"Oh, then I suppose that you are the mother mole," said Tommy Smith.

"Yes, I am," said the mole; "and you should call me Mrs. Mole, and not Mr. as you have been doing; and as for my being like a person, why, I am one, of course, and an important person too, *I* think. Why, do you know that I drain the land?"

"Do you really, Mrs. Mole?" said Tommy Smith; "but is not that very difficult?"

"You would find it so, I daresay,"

answered the mole, "but to me it is quite easy."

"How do you do it?" asked Tommy Smith.

"Why, by digging to be sure," the mole said. "I just make my tunnels, and my trenches, and my corridors, and then when the rain comes it runs off into them, and doesn't lie on the ground so long as it would if they were not there."

"Oh, but if the water runs into your tunnels," said Tommy Smith, "how is it that you are not drowned?"

"Oh, it does not stay there long enough for that," said the mole; "and, besides, I am a very good swimmer. Just take me up again and put me into that little pond there, and I will show you,"—for there was a pond not far off where some ducks and geese were swimming about. "Drive those rude things away first," said the mother mole, as Tommy Smith stood with her in his hand, at the edge of the pond, just ready to drop her in. "If they see me, they will be sure to make some rude remark, and, indeed, there is no saying what liberties they might take."

So Tommy Smith drove away the ducks and geese, and then dropped the mother mole into the water, and,—would you believe it?—she swam almost as well as if she had been a duck or a goose herself, moving all her four little feet at a great rate, and going along very quickly. She *did* look so funny. She went across the pond, and then turned round and came back again, and, as she scuttled out on to the bank, she said, "So now you see that a mole can swim. Can *you*?"

"No," answered Tommy Smith; for he had not learnt to, yet.

"Dear me," said the mother mole, "you cannot swim, or dig, or drain the ground, and I am so much smaller and can do all three, besides a great many other things. But then *I* am a mole."

"I didn't say that I couldn't dig," Tommy Smith said. "I can, a little, only *I* do it with a spade. I mean a real spade," he added. "Of course, I can't do it with my hands."

"What stupid hands!" said the mole. "Why, what *can* they be good for? But are you sure you could dig properly, even if you had a spade? Do you think you could do anything useful now? For instance, could you dig a well?"

"I shouldn't like to do it all by myself,"

said Tommy Smith; "it would take me a very long time. But I don't suppose *you* dig wells either."

"Oh, don't you!" said the mole; "then how do you think we get our water to drink when the weather is dry? Of course, if we have a pond or a ditch near us we can easily make a tunnel to the edge of it, but it is not every mole who is so fortunate as to live by the waterside. Those who do not, have to dig deep pits for the water to run into; for I must tell you that there is always water to be found in the earth, if only you dig deep enough for it. If you make a hole which goes right down into the ground, very soon the water will begin to trickle into it through the sides and the bottom, and then, of course, it is a well. I wish you could see some of our wells. They are so nicely made, and sometimes they are brim full."

"So you have real wells with water in them!" cried Tommy Smith; for it seemed to him so very funny that moles should have wells as well as men.

"To be sure, we have," said the mole; "and I think it is very clever of us to have thought of it."

"Yes, it is indeed," said Tommy Smith; "and I begin to think that all the animals are clever."

"I don't know about *that*," said the mole; "but *we* are."

"Oh yes; and so is the rat, and the frog, and the peewit, and "—

"I am glad to hear it," said the mole. "*I* should not have thought so."

"Oh! but they are really," Tommy Smith went on eagerly. "Do let me tell you how the peewit "—

"I have nothing to learn from *him*, I hope," said the mole; "a poor foolish bird who wastes all his time in the air."

"Oh, but if you only knew how the mother peewit"—Tommy Smith was beginning again.

"I should be sorry to take *her* as an example," said the mole sharply; "she is a flighty thing, without solid qualities. Other animals may be all very well in their way," she went on, after a pause, "but they are not *moles*, and they none of them know how to dig."

"Oh, but the rabbit."—

"The rabbit, indeed!" cried the mole very indignantly. "Why, what can *he* do?

He can just make a clumsy hole, and that is all. He is a mere labourer; and I hope you do not compare him with a real artist like myself."

"Oh no," said Tommy Smith; but he thought the mole was very conceited.

"Not that it is his fault," the mole continued. "Of course, he cannot be expected to make such wonderful places as I do. After all, what has he got to dig with? His feet are only paws, they are not spades, as mine are; and then he has two great big eyes for the dirt to get into, which must be a great inconvenience to him."

"But haven't you eyes, too, Mrs. Mole?" asked Tommy Smith.

"Would you like to try and find them?" answered the mole. "You may, if you like."

So Tommy Smith knelt down on the ground and began to look all about where he thought the mole's eyes were likely to be, and to feel with his fingers in the fur. But look and feel as he might, it was no use, he couldn't find the eyes anywhere. But, just as he was going to give up trying, all at once he thought he saw two little black things hardly so big as the head of a small black pin. Could those be eyes? Tommy Smith hardly believed that they could be, for some time; they were so *very* small. "Are those your eyes, Mrs. Mole?" he asked at last.

"Yes, indeed they are," the mother mole answered; "and are they not a beautiful pair? How difficult they are to find, and how well my fur hides them! It would not be easy for the mould to get into *them*; *they* are not like those great staring things of the rabbit."

"They are very small," said Tommy Smith.

"I should think so!" said the mole; "and what an advantage it is to have small eyes."

"But can you see with them?" said Tommy Smith.

"Oh no," said the mole; "and what an advantage it is not to be able to see."

Tommy Smith did not understand this at all. "The rabbit can see," he said, "and so can all the other animals."

"*They* are obliged to," answered the mole, "and so they have to put up with it;

but a mole lives in the dark, and therefore it does not require to see."

"But what are eyes for, if they are not to see with?" Tommy Smith asked. He felt sure it was a sensible question, and it seemed to him that the mole was talking nonsense.

"They are for not getting in the way when you make tunnels in the ground," said the mole. "Mine never get in the way, so I know that they are the best eyes that anyone can have."

This was quite a new idea to Tommy Smith, and he tried to think what it would be like to live in the ground, and to have eyes that you couldn't see with, and that didn't get in the way. At last he said, "It seems to me, Mrs. Mole, that it would be much better if you had not any eyes at all."

"That is a strange idea, to be sure!" said the mole. "Not have eyes, indeed! That would be a fine thing."

"But if you can't see with them," said Tommy Smith.

"What of that?" said the mole; "we have them, and so we are proud of them. It is a saying in our family that a mole *may* be blind, but he has *eyes* for all that."

"Poor little mole," said Tommy Smith, for though the animal seemed to be quite happy itself, he couldn't help feeling very sorry for it. "But are you *quite* blind?"

"If I am not quite, I am very nearly," the mole answered, "and I am thankful for *that*. I just know when it is light and when it isn't, which is all a mole requires to know."

"But can't you see me?" Tommy Smith asked.

"You, indeed!" answered the mole. "And why should I want to see you?"

"I'm afraid you *are* blind," Tommy Smith said quite sadly.

"At anyrate," said the mole, "I have less seeing to do than almost any other animal, and, when I think of that, I can't *help* feeling proud, though I know I oughtn't to be. But I think you have talked enough about my eyes," the mole continued. "Perhaps you would like to know something about my teeth now. Look! there they are," and she opened her mouth as wide as she could, which was not very wide, for her mouth was so small. What funny little white teeth they were, and how sharp,—as sharp and as pointed as needles.

"Why are they so pointed?" asked Tommy Smith. "The rabbit's teeth are not at all like that, and the rat's are not either."

"It is because we eat different things," said the mole. "Different kinds of animals have different food, and so they have different kinds of teeth to eat it with. Mine are nice and sharp, because they have to bite and kill whatever they catch hold of."

"But what is it that they have to bite and kill?" said Tommy Smith.

"Ah, you would never guess," answered the mole. "You must know that we moles are very brave animals, and we fight a great deal; sometimes with each other, but mostly with great serpents which live in the ground, although it really belongs to us."

"Serpents?" said Tommy Smith. "Why, do you mean snakes?"

"Of course I do," said the mole.

"Snakes that live in the ground!" Tommy Smith cried. "Why, I don't

"WE MOLES ARE VERY HEROIC"

THE MOLE

know of any that do. The grass-snake doesn't, or the adder either. What are these snakes like, Mrs. Mole?"

"They are smooth and slimy," said the mole. "They have no head, or, if they have, it looks like another tail, and they are always crawling through the ground, which is ours, of course, and trying to break into our palaces."

"Oh, but I call those worms!" said Tommy Smith.

"You may call them so if you like," said the mole, "but *I* call them snakes. You should see the way I fight with them! How they writhe and twist about when I seize them between my sharp teeth. They try hard to get away, and they would kill me if only they could. But I am too brave and too strong for them, so I kill *them* instead, and eat them as well. We moles are very heroic."

"Do you eat anything else?" asked Tommy Smith.

"Caterpillars sometimes, and a beetle or two," answered the mole. "But *I* like snakes best of all."

"Worms," said Tommy Smith.

"Snakes," said the mole. But Tommy Smith was right, the mole's snakes were harmless worms; but it is nice to think oneself a hero.

"Good-bye," said the mole rather suddenly. "I am tired of talking, and I want to have a little sleep."

"Oh, but it is the middle of the day," said Tommy Smith.

"What of that?" said the mole. "I feel tired, so I shall go to sleep."

"Then do you always sleep in the daytime?" asked Tommy Smith.

"I know nothing about daytime or nighttime," the mole answered, "and perhaps if you lived under the ground, as I do, you would not either. I feel tired *now*, so I shall go to sleep now. Good-bye"; and the mother mole began to sink into the earth, and all at once she was gone,—just as Tommy Smith was going to ask her what was the use of having such a grand palace to live in if she was blind and couldn't see it.

One sometimes thinks of a good question just too late to ask it.

CHAPTER IX.

THE WOODPIGEON

*"The woodpigeon greets Tommy Smith with a coo,
Which he modifies slightly to 'How do you do?'"*

WHAT could be more beautiful than the woods that fine spring morning on which Tommy Smith walked through them? The sky was blue, and the air was soft, and the birds were singing everywhere. There was a concert, surely; the trees had given it. That is what came into Tommy Smith's head, and perhaps he was right. It is in spring that the season begins. Then ladies and gentlemen dress themselves finely, and come and stand together in a crowd, and there is talking, and laughing, and singing. And here in the woods the trees had all put on fine new dresses of bright green, for *their* season of spring had come, and green was the fashionable colour. *They* stood together too,—ever so many of them,—and bent their heads towards each other, and seemed to be whispering. Then their leaves rustled, which was a much pleasanter sound than ladies' and gentlemen's talking and laughing (though perhaps it did not mean *quite* as much); and, oh! what beautiful sounds came from their midst. Tommy Smith knew that it was not the trees who were singing, but the birds in them. "But it seems as if it were the trees," he thought, "because I can't see the birds. But perhaps the trees ask the birds to sing for them, as we ask people to play and sing for us. That is how they give their concerts and parties, perhaps. The large ones are like rich people who can afford to hire a whole band, but the little ones and the bushes are the people who are not so well off, and *they* can only have a bird or two." Tommy Smith thought all this, because he was a little boy, and liked to pretend things, but a long time afterwards, when he was much wiser, he used to remember those walks of his in the woods, and sometimes he would say to himself, "Yes, those were the best seasons; those were the concerts and parties most worth going to."

THE WOODPIGEON

A fallen tree lay across Tommy Smith's path. It had once been a tall, stately oak, now it made a nice mossy seat for a little boy. We are not all of us so useful when we grow old. "I will sit down on it," thought Tommy Smith, "and listen to the birds singing, and pretend they are people, and not birds at all." So Tommy Smith sat down and listened. A thrush was sitting on the very tip-top of a high fir tree, and soon he began to fill the whole air with his beautiful, clear, joyous notes. "I like that as well as the piano," said Tommy Smith, "and I don't think I know any lady who could sing such a beautiful song." Then the robin began. "That is lower and sweeter," he thought. "*People* make a great deal more noise when they sing, but it doesn't seem to mean so much, or, if it does, I don't like the meaning so well. Then a jay screamed, and some starlings began to chatter. "Oh, there!" cried Tommy Smith, clapping his hands. "That is much more like people. Ladies talk and sing just like that. But not like *that*," he continued; for now another sound began to mingle with the rest, such a pretty, such a *very* pretty sound, *so* soft, and so tender and sleepy, "like a lullaby," Tommy Smith thought. And, as he listened to it, all the woods seemed to grow hushed and still, as if they were listening too. "Oh," said Tommy Smith, "it is no use pretending any more. That couldn't be people. No men, and no women either, have such a pretty voice as that."

"Coo-oo-oo-oo, coo-oo-oo-oo," said the voice. It had been some way off before, but now it sounded much nearer. "Coo-oo-oo-oo, coo-oo-oo-oo." Why, surely it was in that tree, only just a little way from where Tommy Smith was sitting. "I will go and look," he thought. "I know who it is. It is the woodpigeon. Perhaps he will stay and talk to me."

So he got up, and walked towards the tree. But—was it not strange?—as he came to it the voice seemed to change just a little. Only just a little; it had still the same pretty, soft sound, and the end part was just the same, but, instead of "Coo-oo-oo-oo, coo-oo-oo-oo," which it had been saying before, now it was saying—yes, and quite distinctly too—" How do you do-oo-oo-oo? How do you do-oo-oo-oo?" Yes,

THE WOODPIGEON

there could be no doubt of it, and as Tommy Smith came quite up to the tree, there was the woodpigeon sitting on one of the lowest branches, bowing to him quite politely, and asking him how he was.

"Oh, I am quite well, Mr. Woodpigeon," answered Tommy Smith. "I hope you are."

"Oh, I am quite well too-oo-oo-oo," cooed the woodpigeon, bobbing his head up and down all the while.

"Why do you move your head up and down like that whilst you speak?" asked Tommy Smith.

"Why, because it is the proper thing to do-oo-oo-oo," replied the woodpigeon.

"But *I* don't do it when *I* speak," said Tommy Smith.

"Oh no; but then *I* am not you-oo-oo-oo," said the woodpigeon.

Tommy Smith didn't know how to answer this, so he thought he would change the subject. "What have you been doing this morning, Mr. Woodpigeon?" he said.

"Why, sitting here in the woo-oo-oo-oods and coo-oo-oo-ing," the woodpigeon answered.

"Oh, but not all the morning, have you?" said Tommy Smith.

"Oh no," said the woodpigeon. "From about six to nine I was having my breakfast in the fields."

Tommy Smith thought that three hours was a very long time to take over one's breakfast, and he said so. "I don't take half an hour over mine," he added.

"That is all very well," said the woodpigeon; "but your breakfast is brought to you, whilst I have to find mine for myself. What you eat is put down before you on a table, but *my* table is the whole country, and it is so large and broad that it takes me a long while to find what is on it, and to eat as much of it as I want."

"I wonder what your breakfast is like, Mr. Woodpigeon," said Tommy Smith. "I suppose it is very different to mine."

"Let me see," cooed the woodpigeon. "This morning I had a few peas and beans, besides some oats and barley. I got those in the fields, and I found some green clover there too, as well as some wild mustard, and some ragweed and charlock, and a few other seeds and roo-oo-oo-oots."

"Oh dear, Mr. Woodpigeon," said Tommy Smith; "why, what a lot you do eat."

"I don't call that much," said the woodpigeon. "When I was tired of looking about in the fields, I went to the woods again, and got a few acorns, and some beechnuts, and"—

"Oh! but look here, Mr. Woodpigeon," said Tommy Smith. "You couldn't have eaten all those this morning, because they are not all ripe now, and"—

"I didn't say they were ripe," said the woodpigeon; "and if I didn't eat them this morning, then I did on some other morning, so it's all the same. Those are the things I eat, at anyrate, and I can't be expected to remember exactly when I eat them. I had a few stones though, of course. They are always to be had, whatever time of year it is. *Stones* are *always* in season."

"Stones!" cried Tommy Smith in great surprise. "Oh, come now; I know you don't eat them."

"Oh, don't I?" said the woodpigeon. "I should be very sorry if I couldn't get any,—I know that. It would be a nice thing, indeed, if one couldn't have a few stones to eat with one's meals. That would be a good joke."

Tommy Smith thought that *he* wouldn't think it a joke to *have* to eat stones, and he could hardly believe that the woodpigeon was speaking the truth. But he was such an innocent-looking bird, and seemed so *very* respectable, that he thought he must be. "Are they very large stones?" he asked at last.

"Oh no," answered the woodpigeon. "They are not large, but very small—just the right size to go into my mill."

"Into your mill?" said Tommy Smith.

"Yes," said the woodpigeon; "the little mill which is inside me."

Tommy Smith was getting more and more puzzled. What could the woodpigeon mean? "And yet he is such a nice bird," he said to himself. "I do 't think he would tell stories."

"I see that you don't understand me," said the woodpigeon; "so, if you like, I will explain it all to you."

"Oh, I should so like to know!" said Tommy Smith.

So the woodpigeon gave a gentle coo,

and began to tell him all about it. "Yes," he said, "I have a mill inside me, and everything that I eat goes into it to get ground up."

"Why, then, you are a miller," said Tommy Smith.

"In a way, I am," said the woodpigeon; "for I own a mill. But then, you know, a miller lives inside *his* mill, but *my* mill is inside me."

"I should so like to see it," said Tommy Smith.

"You never can do that," said the woodpigeon in an alarmed tone of voice; "for you would have to kill me first, and that would be a most shocking thing to do. But it is there, all the same, though you can't see it, and it is called the gizzard."

"Oh, the gizzard!" said Tommy Smith. "I know what that is, because I have"—and then he stopped all of a sudden. He had been going to say that he had tasted it sometimes when there was fowl for dinner, but he thought he had better not. It didn't seem quite delicate to talk to a woodpigeon about eating a fowl.

"The gizzard is the mill that I am talking about," said the woodpigeon.

"All the food that we eat goes into it, and then it is ground up, just as corn is ground between two hard stones. But though our gizzard is very hard, it is not quite so hard as stones are, so we swallow some small sharp stones, which go into our gizzard, and are rolled about with the grain and seeds there, and help to crush them. Then, when they are nice and soft, they are ready to go on into the stomach. So now you know what sort of thing a gizzard is, and why we swallow stones."

"But don't the stones hurt you?" asked Tommy Smith.

"Do you think we would swallow them if they did?" answered the woodpigeon. "What a foolish question to ask!"

Tommy Smith stood for a little while thinking about it, and wondering if *he* had a mill inside *him*, till at last the woodpigeon said, "Perhaps you would like to ask me a *sensible* question."

"Oh yes," said Tommy Smith, and he tried to think what was a sensible question. He had thought of a good many questions to ask, and they had seemed sensible at the time, but now he began to feel afraid that the woodpigeon would think them foolish. At last he said, "Please, Mr. Woodpigeon, where do you live?"

"Oh, in this tree," said the woodpigeon, "half-way up on the seventeenth storey."

"I suppose you mean the seventeenth branch," said Tommy Smith.

"Of course I do," said the woodpigeon. "I have my nest there, and my wife is sitting on the eggs now."

"Oh, do let me see them," cried Tommy Smith.

"Oh no," said the woodpigeon. "They are too high up for that. You would not be able to climb so far, and you cannot fly as we birds do, for you are only a poor boy, and have no wings."

"I wish I had wings," said Tommy Smith. "Is it very nice to fly, Mr. Woodpigeon?"

"It is nicer than anything else in the whole world," the woodpigeon answered. "Just fancy floating along high above everything, as if the air were water, and you were a boat. Only you go much quicker than a boat does, and sometimes you need not use the oars at all."

"Your wings are the oars, I suppose," said Tommy Smith.

"Yes, indeed," said the woodpigeon, "and how fast they row me along. Swish! swish! swish! and when I am tired I just spread them out and float along without using them. That is delightful. I call it resting on my wings."

"It must be something like swinging, I think," said Tommy Smith.

"Yes," said the woodpigeon; "only you swing upon nothing, and you only swing forwards. Oh, how cool and fresh the air is, even on the hottest day in summer! The sun seems shining quite near to me, and the sky is like a great blue sea that I am swimming through; but oh, so quickly! quicker than any fish can swim. When I look up, I see great white ships with all their sails set. They are the clouds, and sometimes I am quite near them. How fast we go! We seem to be chasing each other. And when I look down, I see green islands far below me. Those are the tops of trees that I am flying over. My nest is in one of them, and I always know which one it is. When I am above it, I pause as a boat pauses on the crest of a wave, and then down, down, down I go, such a deep, cool, delicious plunge, till at last the leaves rustle round me, and I am sitting amongst the branches again, and cooing."

"By your nest?" asked Tommy Smith.

"Oh yes; when I have one," said the woodpigeon. "I have now, you know, because it is the springtime."

"I wish I could see it with the eggs in it," said Tommy Smith. But it was no use wishing, he hadn't wings, and he couldn't climb the tree. "How many eggs are there?" he asked.

"Two-oo-oo-oo," said a voice, higher up amongst the foliage; and Tommy Smith knew that the mother woodpigeon was sitting there on her nest, and looking down at him all the while.

"Only two eggs!" he said. "I don't call that many."

"It may not be *many*," said the mother woodpigeon, "but it is the right quantity. Three would be *too* many, and one would not be enough. Two is the only possible number."

"Oh no, indeed it isn't," said Tommy Smith eagerly. "Fowls lay a dozen eggs sometimes, and pheasants"—

"Possible for a woodpigeon, *I* meant," said the mother woodpigeon. "With fowls, no doubt, anything may take place, but large families are considered vulgar amongst *us*."

"Fowls may do what they please," said the father woodpigeon. "They are lazy birds, and don't feed their young ones."

"That is why they lay so many eggs," said the mother woodpigeon. "They don't mind having a herd of children, because they know they won't have to support them."

Tommy Smith was surprised to hear the woodpigeons talk like this of the poor fowls, for he had often seen the good mother hen walking about with her brood of children, calling to them when she found a worm, and taking care of them so nicely. "It seems to me," he thought, "that every animal thinks itself better than every other animal; and they all think whatever they do right, just because they do it, and the others don't. But I suppose *that* is because they *are* animals, and not human beings." Then he said out loud, "But I am sure the mother hen feeds her chickens, because

I have seen her scratching up worms for them out of the ground, and "—

"Yes, that is a nice way to feed one's little ones," said the mother woodpigeon. "A raw, live worm! Why, what could be nastier? No wonder they are forced to pick up things for themselves."

"If they waited till their parents put a worm into their mouths, they would starve," said the father woodpigeon. "It is quite dreadful to think of."

"But I think the little chickens like picking up their own food," said Tommy Smith. "They look so pretty running about."

"They would look much prettier sitting in a warm nest, as ours do," said the mother woodpigeon.

"And they would feel much more comfortable with you feeding them, my dear," said the father.

"And with you helping me, you know," said the mother bird, and she stretched her neck over the branch, and cooed softly to her husband, who looked up at her, and cooed again.

"Then do you both feed them?" asked Tommy Smith.

"Yes," said the father woodpigeon; "and we take it in turns. You would not find many cocks who would do that, I think."

"No; or help to hatch the eggs," said the mother woodpigeon. "He does that too. Oh, he *is* so good!"

"Nonsense!" said the father woodpigeon. "It is what all birds ought to do-oo-oo-oo."

"Yes; but it isn't what they all do do-oo-oo-oo," said the mother woodpigeon.

"More shame for those who do not," said the father woodpigeon; "but I hope there are not many." And then they both waited for Tommy Smith to ask them another question.

"Please, Mrs. Woodpigeon," said Tommy Smith, "what do you feed your young ones with?"

"We feed them with whatever we eat ourselves," said the mother woodpigeon, "and we always swallow it first, to be sure that it is quite good."

This surprised Tommy Smith very much indeed, for it seemed to him almost as wonderful as eating stones. "Oh! but if you swallow the food your-

THE WOODPIGEON

selves," he said, "how can your young ones have it?"

"They don't have it till we bring it up again," said the father woodpigeon. "They put their beaks inside ours, and then it comes up into our mouths all ready for them to swallow."

"Isn't that rather nasty?" said Tommy Smith.

"You had better ask *them* about *that*," said the mother woodpigeon. "*They* will tell you whether it is nasty or not."

"*They* think it *nice*," said the father woodpigeon.

"And no wonder," said the mother woodpigeon. "When *we* swallow it, it is hard and cold, but when it comes up again for *them* to swallow, it is soft and warm, and very like milk. It is not every bird who feeds its young ones like *that*."

"Oh no," said Tommy Smith; "most birds fly to them with a worm or a caterpillar in their beaks, and give it to them just as it is."

"That is the old-fashioned way," said the mother woodpigeon; "but we are more civilised, and have learnt to *prepare* our children's food."

"Besides," said the father woodpigeon, "we eat seeds and grains, and little things like that, and it would take us a very long time to carry a sufficient number of them to the nest. Our young ones would be so hungry, and we should not be able to bring them enough to satisfy them, and then they would starve. So we have thought of this way of managing it, and I think it is one of the cleverest things in the whole world."

"Yes, indeed," cooed the mother woodpigeon, as she looked down from the branch where she sat on her nest; "one of the cleverest things in the whole world."

"Is it only pigeons that do that?" asked Tommy Smith.

"I won't say that," answered the mother woodpigeon. "There are some other birds, I believe, who have followed our example."

"Yes, they imitate us," said the father woodpigeon; "but they can never be pigeons, however much they try to be."

"Never," said the mother woodpigeon. "They don't drink water as we do. That is the test."

"Why, how do you drink water?" asked

Tommy Smith. "Don't you drink it like other birds?"

"I should think not," said the father woodpigeon. "Other birds take a little in their bills, and then lift their heads up and let it run down their throats, but we pigeons would be ashamed to drink in such a way as that. We keep our beaks in the water all the time, and suck it up into our throats. That is how *we* drink, and nothing could make us do it differently. We don't lift *our* heads up."

"But why shouldn't you lift them up?" said Tommy Smith; for he thought to himself, "If all the other birds drink like that, it ought to be the right way."

"Why shouldn't we?" said the father woodpigeon. "Why, because it would be stupid,—and wrong too," he added after a pause, during which he seemed to be thinking.

"There is a still stronger reason," said the mother woodpigeon, "the strongest of *all* reasons; at least, *I* cannot imagine one stronger. It would be *unpigeonly*." And from the tone in which she said this, Tommy Smith felt that it would be no use to say anything more on the subject.

"If there was any water here," said the father woodpigeon, "I would drink a little just to show you, but the nearest is some way off. However, you can watch some tame pigeons the next time they are drinking, for we all belong to one great family, and have the same ideas upon important points. Now I am going for a short fly, but if you like to stay and talk to my wife, I shall be back again in an hour."

But Tommy Smith had to go too, for his lessons began at eleven o'clock, and of course it would not do to miss them, though it seemed to him that he was getting a much better lesson from the woodpigeons. "But I wish," he said, "before you fly away, Mr. Woodpigeon, you would just tell me what you do all day." But as Tommy Smith said this, there was a rustle and a clapping of wings, and the father woodpigeon was gone.

"He is so impetuous," said the mother woodpigeon. "There is no stopping him when he wants to do anything. But *I* will tell you what we do all day, so listen. We rise early, of course, and fly down to breakfast at about six. After three or four hours we come back to the woods again, and coo and talk to each other there for about an hour. Then we go off to drink and to bathe, which is the nicest part of the whole day. After that we feel a little tired and sleepy, so we sit quietly in the woods till about two. Then it is quite time for dinner, so off we go again and feed till about five. After dinner it is best to sit quiet and coo a little. A quiet coo aids digestion. Then we have a nice refreshing drink in the cool of the evening, and after that we go straight to tree."

"Do you mean to bed?" said Tommy Smith.

"Of course I do," said the mother woodpigeon. "We sleep in trees. They are the only beds we should care to trust ourselves to."

"Aren't they rather hard?" said Tommy Smith.

"Not at all," said the woodpigeon. "You see, we have our own feathers, so that makes them feather-beds. They are soft enough and warm enough for us, you may be quite sure."

"But it must be very windy up in the trees," said Tommy Smith.

"That is the great advantage of the situation," said the mother woodpigeon. "Our beds are always well aired, so we need never feel anxious about that. However much it rains they can never be damp, for how can a bed be damp and well-aired at the same time?"

Tommy Smith couldn't think of the right answer to this, and the woodpigeon went on, "So, now, I have told you how we pass the day. What a happy, happy life! He must have a cruel heart who could put an end to it." (And Tommy Smith thought so too.)

"But is that what you always do?" he asked.

"Of course, when there are eggs and young ones it makes a difference," said the mother woodpigeon; "and in winter we keep different hours. But that is our usual summer life, and *I* think it a very pleasant one."

"Oh, so do I!" said Tommy Smith. "Thank you, Mrs. Woodpigeon, for telling me. Now I must go to my lessons, and I will tell them all about it at home."

"If you come back afterwards, I will tell

you some more," said the mother woodpigeon.

Tommy Smith said he would, and then he ran away as fast as he could to his lessons, for he was a little late. And as he ran, he could hear the mother woodpigeon saying, "Come back soo-oo-oo-oon! come back soo-oo-oo-oon!"

CHAPTER X.

THE SQUIRREL

*"The pert little squirrel's as brisk as can be;
He calls his house 'Tree-tops,' and lives in a tree."*

SO Tommy Smith went home to his lessons, and when he had finished them, he put on his hat and came out again, and began to walk through the woods to where the mother woodpigeon was waiting for him on her nest. "Tommy Smith! Tommy Smith! Where are you going to, Tommy Smith?" said a voice which he had not heard before. At anyrate, he had not heard it talk before. Such a funny little voice it was, something between a cough and a sob, and if it had not said all those words so *very* distinctly, it would have sounded like "sug, sug,—sug, sug,—sug, sug, sug, sug, sug." Now I come to think of it, Tommy Smith must have heard it before, for he had often been for walks in the woods. But when a voice which has only said "sug, sug" before, begins to talk and say whole sentences, it

THE SQUIRREL

is not so easy to recognise it. "Who can that be?" said Tommy Smith; and then he looked all about, but he could see no one. "Who are you?" he called out; "and where are you calling me from?"

"From here, Tommy Smith, from here," answered the voice. "Can't you see me? Why here I am."

"Are you the rabbit?" said Tommy Smith; but he thought directly, "Oh no, it can't be the rabbit, because it comes from a tree, and no rabbit could burrow up a tree."

"The rabbit, indeed!" said the voice. "Oh no, I am not the rabbit. That *is* a funny sug, sug, sug, sug-gestion."

"Oh, I know!" cried Tommy Smith. "It is the "—

"Look!" said the voice. And all at once there was a red streak down the trunk of a beech tree and along the ground, and there was a little squirrel sitting at Tommy Smith's feet, with his tail cocked up over his head. "Oh!" cried Tommy Smith,—and before he could say anything else the squirrel said "Look!" again, and there was another red streak, up the trunk of a pine tree this time,—and there he was sitting on a branch of it, with his tail cocked up over his head, just the same as before.

"Oh dear, Mr. Squirrel," said Tommy Smith—the branch was not a very high one, and they could talk to each other comfortably—"how fast you do go!"

"Oh, I like to do things quickly," said the squirrel. "Mine is an active nature during three-parts of the year."

"And what is it during the other part?" asked Tommy Smith.

"Oh, I don't know anything about it then," the squirrel answered.

This puzzled Tommy Smith a little. "Why not?" he said.

"Oh, because I'm asleep," said the squirrel. "One can't know much about oneself when one's asleep, you know; and, besides, it doesn't matter."

"But do you go to sleep for such a long time?" said Tommy Smith. "I know that the frogs and the snakes go to sleep all the winter, but I didn't know any regular animal did."

"Why, doesn't the dormouse?" said the squirrel. "He's a much harder sleeper than I am. I suppose you call *him* a regular animal.'

"Oh yes," said Tommy Smith. He had forgotten the dormouse, and, of course, *he was* a regular animal. By a "regular animal," I suppose Tommy Smith meant one that wasn't an insect, or a reptile, or a worm, or something of that sort. Perhaps he couldn't have said exactly *what* he meant, but whatever he did mean, you may be sure that it was not very sensible, because all living creatures are animals, and one is just as regular as another, if you look at it in the right way.

"Well," said the squirrel, "I think we are to have a little chat, are we not? It's you that must ask the questions, you know."

"Oh, I should so like to," said Tommy Smith, "but I promised the mother woodpigeon to go back and talk to her, and I am going there now."

"The mother woodpigeon will be on her nest for another hour or two," said the squirrel, "so you will have time to talk to her and to me too. And let me tell you, it is not every little boy who can have a talk with a squirrel."

Tommy Smith thought that it was not every little boy who could have a talk with a woodpigeon either. But he wanted to have both, so he said, "Very well, Mr. Squirrel, and I hope you will tell me something interesting about yourself."

The squirrel only nodded, and said nothing; and then Tommy Smith remembered that he had to ask the questions, so he said, "Why is it, Mr. Squirrel, that you go to sleep in the winter? It seems so funny that you should. I stay awake all the time, you know—except at night, of course,—so why can't you?"

"That is easily answered," said the squirrel. "You have food in the winter, don't you?"

"Oh yes," said Tommy Smith.

"Of course you do," said the squirrel. "It is all got for you, so you have no trouble. *I* have to find mine myself, but in the winter there is none to find. So if I didn't go to sleep, I should starve."

Tommy Smith remembered, then, that the grass-snake had told him that *he* went to sleep in the winter, because he could get no frogs to eat; and the frog had said *he* did, because he could find no insects. So he saw that there was the same reason for all these three animals, who were so different from each other, doing the same thing. "And that's why the dormouse goes to sleep too, I suppose," he said to himself, and then he began to think that if any other animals went to sleep all the winter, it must be because *they* could get no food.

"But I don't think *I could* go to sleep if I was very hungry," he said to the squirrel; "and if I did, I'm sure I should wake up again very soon and want my dinner."

"I daresay you would," said the squirrel; "and if you couldn't get it, you would soon die."

"But do *you* never wake up and want *your* dinner, Mr. Squirrel?" said Tommy Smith.

"Oh yes," said the squirrel, "I often wake up, but whenever I do, I can always get it. Do you know why? Because I am such a clever animal, that I hide away food in the autumn, so that I can find it in the winter."

"But you *said* you couldn't find food in the winter," said Tommy Smith.

"Oh, I meant that I couldn't find it growing on the trees and bushes," said the squirrel. "Of course I can find what I have stored away, and that is enough for all the time I am awake. But it wouldn't be enough for the whole winter, so I sleep or doze most of the time, and then I don't require anything."

"But why don't you store away enough food for the whole winter?" said Tommy Smith. "Then you needn't go to sleep at all, you know."

"Good gracious!" said the squirrel, "that would take a great deal too much time. It is all very well to put a few things aside, so as to have something to eat on sunny days—for those are the days I like to wake up on,—but just fancy having to find dinners beforehand for every day all through the winter. I could never do that, you know. One dinner to think about is quite enough as a rule. How should you like to have to cook two dinners every day, and always put one of them in a cupboard?"

"But you don't *cook your* dinners, Mr. Squirrel," said Tommy Smith.

"And *you* don't *look* for *yours*," said the squirrel. "*I* do. You see," he went on, "I only begin hiding things away towards the end of autumn, so there isn't so very much time."

"But you have the rest of the year to do it in too," said Tommy Smith.

"Oh no," said the squirrel; "that's quite a mistake. In the spring and summer I have something else to think about. Besides, there is nothing worth hiding away then—no acorns, or beechnuts, or filberts, and, of course, one wants to have something really nice to eat when one wakes up in the winter. But in the autumn all those things are ripe. The autumn is the great eating-time. That is the time of the year that I like best of all."

"What! better than the spring or the summer?" said Tommy Smith.

"Well, in the spring there are buds on the trees," the squirrel reflected; "and the birds' nests have got eggs inside them. They are both very nice, though I like nuts better still. But, you see, buds and birds' eggs don't keep, and so"—

"Oh but, Mr. Squirrel," cried Tommy Smith, "you surely don't eat the eggs of the poor birds! Oh, I hope you don't!" (You see he was not at all the same Tommy Smith now that he used to be, and he didn't go birds'-nesting any more.)

The squirrel looked just a little bit

ashamed. "I wouldn't, you know," he said, "if they didn't make their nests in the trees."

"Of course they make their nests in the trees!" said Tommy Smith indignantly. "They have just as much right to the trees as you have, and I think it is very wicked of you to eat their eggs."

"Perhaps it is," said the squirrel; "but, you see, I get so hungry, and fresh eggs are so nice. By the bye, on what tree did you say the woodpigeon was sitting? I think I will go there with you."

"*Indeed*, you shan't!" said Tommy Smith (and he was *very* angry). "I won't take you there. You want to eat her eggs, I know; and I think you are a very naughty animal."

The squirrel looked at Tommy Smith for a little while without speaking, and then he said, "You know, *I* never eat hen's eggs."

"Don't you?" said Tommy Smith. It was all he could think of to say, for he remembered that *he did* eat hen's eggs. Of course he knew that that was different—the peewit had told him that it was—but just at that moment he couldn't think of

THE SQUIRREL

why it was different, and he couldn't help wishing that he hadn't been *quite* so angry with the squirrel. "Perhaps you don't eat too many eggs," he said in a milder tone.

"Of course not," said the squirrel. "Wherever there are plenty of squirrels, there are plenty of birds too, as long as people with guns don't shoot them. That shows that we don't eat too many. And then, as for our killing trees"—

"Oh, but *do* you kill trees?" said Tommy Smith. "I didn't know that you did that."

"Why, sometimes when we are very hungry," said the squirrel, "we gnaw the bark all round the trunk of a small tree, and then it dies. So those people who are always finding out reasons for killing animals say we do harm to the forests. But I can tell them this, that no forest was ever cut down by the squirrels that lived in it. Men cut down the forests, and shoot the birds and the squirrels; but if they left them all three alone, they would all get on very well together. Once, you know, almost the whole of England was covered with forests. Do you think it was the squirrels who cut them all down?"

"Oh no," said Tommy Smith. "It was men with axes, I should think."

"Yes," said the squirrel. "It is that great axe of theirs that does the mischief, not these poor little teeth of mine. It is axes, not squirrels, that they should keep out of the woods."

Tommy Smith thought the squirrel might be right, but he wanted to hear something more about what he did and the way he lived, so he said, "Oh, Mr. Squirrel, you haven't told me where you hide the nuts and acorns that you eat when you wake up in the winter."

"Oh, in all sorts of places," said the squirrel. "Sometimes I scrape a hole in the ground and bury them in it, and sometimes I put them into holes in the trunks of trees, or under their roots, if they run along the ground, or into any other little nook or crevice near where I live. In fact, I put them anywhere where it is convenient, but *not* where it is *in*convenient. That is another of my clever notions."

"But isn't it rather difficult to find them again when you wake up a long time afterwards?" said Tommy Smith.

"It would be to you, I daresay," said

the squirrel; "but it is quite easy to me. You see, I have a wonderful memory, and never forget where I once put a thing. Even when the snow is on the ground, I know where my dinner is. It is *under* a white tablecloth then, instead of being *upon* one. I have only to lift up the tablecloth, and there it is."

"Do you mean that you scrape the snow away, Mr. Squirrel?" said Tommy Smith.

"Yes, that is what I mean," said the squirrel; "but I like to talk prettily. Well, have you anything else to ask me? You had better make haste if you have, because we squirrels can never stay still for very long, and I shall soon have to jump away. Look how my tail is whisking. I always go very soon after that begins."

Tommy Smith thought that, as the squirrel had proposed having a chat himself, and had prevented him from going on to the woodpigeon, it was not quite polite of him to be so very impatient. But he thought *he* would be polite, at anyrate, so he went on, all in a hurry, " I suppose, Mr. Squirrel, as you go to sleep in the winter, you have to come out of the trees and find a place on the ground to "—

"Out of the trees!" exclaimed the squirrel. "I should think not, indeed. That would be very unsafe. Besides, I should never feel comfortable if I did not rock with the wind when I was asleep. I should have a nasty fixed feeling, which would wake me up every minute."

This surprised Tommy Smith a good deal. He knew that squirrels lived in the trees all day, but he did not know before that they slept in them at night too. "Then do you make a nest like a bird, Mr. Squirrel?" he asked.

"Like a bird, indeed!" said the squirrel. "No; I make one like a squirrel. It is not necessary for me to imitate a bird. We squirrels can make nests a great deal better than birds can."

Tommy Smith did not quite believe this. At anyrate, he felt sure that a squirrel could not make a better nest than some birds can. But he remembered that some other birds make only slight nests, or none at all, " And perhaps," he thought, "he only means those kinds of birds." But he thought he had better not ask the

THE SQUIRREL

squirrel this, in case he should be offended, so he only said, "Oh, Mr. Squirrel, will you please tell me all about your nest, and how you make it, and what it looks like."

"Well," the squirrel began, "it is very large; much larger than you would ever think, to look at *me*. I could get inside the cap you have on your head. But how large do you think the house I make, and go to sleep in, is?"

"Perhaps it is a little larger than my cap," said Tommy Smith. He did not think it could be *much* larger.

"Why," said the squirrel, "it is larger than you sometimes. You know those great heaps of hay that stand in the fields—haycocks I think they call them,—well, if you were to take my house to pieces, it would sometimes make a heap almost as big as one of them."

"Would it, really?" said Tommy Smith. "But why is it so large?"

"You see," said the squirrel, "if the walls were not nice and thick, they would not keep out the cold properly, and so I have to find a great deal of moss and grass, and a great many sticks and leaves, to make it with. Then I have to repair it every year—it would be too much trouble, you know, to build a new one,—and so it keeps on getting bigger, because of the fresh sticks and things I bring to it. That is why my house is so large."

"And are you always quite comfortable inside it?" said Tommy Smith.

"Oh yes," said the squirrel; "always comfortable, and always dry. I knit everything so closely together, that neither the rain nor the snow can get through."

"I suppose your house has a door to get in and out by," said Tommy Smith.

"It has *two* doors," said the squirrel, "a large one and a small one. Why, what a question to ask! You will be asking if it has a roof to it next."

"*Has* it a roof?" said Tommy Smith. (So, you see, the squirrel was quite right.)

"Of course it has," said the squirrel. "The idea of living in a house without a roof to it! I build it high up in the fork of a tree," he went on; "and I lie curled up inside it, as snug and as warm as can be."

"But isn't it too warm in the summer?" asked Tommy Smith.

"Oh, I don't go into it then," said the

THE SQUIRREL

squirrel. "The house I have been telling you about is for the winter, but in the summer I have my summer-house to go into."

"Oh, then you have two houses!" said Tommy Smith. "That is cleverer than a bird, for they have only one nest."

"*I* have two," said the squirrel, "and they are not at all the same."

"Oh, do tell me what the summer-house is like," said Tommy Smith.

"It is more lightly built than the winter-house," said the squirrel, "and not nearly so large. That is how summer-houses are always built, you know. Perhaps you have one in your garden."

"Oh yes, we have," said Tommy Smith.

"And isn't it much smaller than the other one?" said the squirrel.

"Oh yes, it is," said Tommy Smith.

"Well," said the squirrel, "my summer-house is constructed on the same principle. I will show it you, if you like, for I really can't sit still any longer. Just *look* at my tail! It will whisk itself off soon if I don't jump about."

"Oh, I should so like to see it, Mr. Squirrel!" cried Tommy Smith. "Yes, do come down, and"—

"Oh, I'm not coming down," said the squirrel. "I shouldn't think of doing that. I shall go home by the treeway, and you can walk underneath me. Now then!" And as the squirrel said this, he gave his tail *such* a whisking, and away he ran along the branch he had been sitting on, right to the end of it, and then gave *such* a jump on to the branch of another tree, and then out of that tree into another one, and so from tree to tree, so fast that Tommy Smith could hardly keep up with him as he ran along the ground underneath.

It was not always that the squirrel had to jump from one tree to another, because their branches often touched each other, and then he would run along them without jumping at all. Sometimes they would be very near together without quite touching, and then when he came to the end of the branch he was on, he would lean forward, and, with his little forepaws, catch hold of the tips of several of those belonging to another tree, and draw them all together, and then give a little spring amongst them, and away he would go again. This was when he was in the fir trees. But to see him run down the long, drooping branch of a beech tree, right to the very end, and then drop off it on to another one far below—that was the finest sight of all. He did it so very gracefully. His tail was not turned up over his back now, as it had been whilst he was sitting up, but went streaming out behind him like a flag. And sometimes he would whisk it from side to side, and say, "Sug, sug,—sug, sug,—sug, sug, sug, sug, sug!"

"Here it is!" cried the squirrel at last, from one of the very top branches of the tree he was on (it was a large beech tree). "Here is 'Tree-tops.' Can you see it?"

"Oh yes, I can see the top of the tree you are on," said Tommy Smith; "but"—

"Oh, I don't mean that!" said the squirrel. "'Tree-tops' is the name of my residence. You know, houses have usually a name of some sort. So I call mine 'Tree-tops.' That describes it very well, because it is in a tree-top, and there are tree-tops all round it."

"But aren't all squirrels' nests like that?" said Tommy Smith.

"Oh yes," said the squirrel; "and they

can all be called 'Tree-tops.' I daresay you've seen more than one house that was named 'The Elms,' or 'The Firs,' or 'The Beeches.' But now look about, and see if you can see my summer-house."

Tommy Smith looked all about near where the squirrel was sitting high up in the tree, and at last he saw something that looked like a little black ball. "Is that it?" he said.

"Yes," said the squirrel, "that's it. Look! Now I am in it," and he made a little spring at the ball of sticks, and disappeared inside it. The jump made the thin end of the branch swing about, and the squirrel's summer-house swung with it, so that it looked as if it might be shaken off.

"Oh, do come out," Tommy Smith cried. "I'm sure it can't be safe in there."

"Not safe!" said the squirrel, as he poked his little head out, and looked down at Tommy Smith. "Do you think I would live with all my family in a house that was not safe? I have a wife and five children, you know, and we all live here together."

"Do you really, Mr. Squirrel?" said Tommy Smith, for he could hardly believe it.

"Why, of course we do," said the squirrel; "and great fun it is, too. You should see how we swing about in a high wind. Delightful!"

Tommy Smith thought that it would make *him* giddy. "It *must* be dangerous," he said. "Suppose you were all to be swung out, or the branch were to be blown off, or"—

"Oh, we never think of such things," said the squirrel. "They are sure not to happen; and even if they did, we should be all right, somehow, I daresay."

"I don't think you would," said Tommy Smith. "The woodpigeon might, perhaps, but, you see, you can't fly, and so"—

"Oh, can't I?" said the squirrel. "Why, how did I get here then, from tree to tree? Didn't you see me?"

"Oh, but that was jumping," said Tommy Smith.

"Jumping? Nonsense!" said the squirrel. "Why, I went through the air, you know, and that is just what one does when one flies, isn't it?"

"Oh yes, of course," said Tommy Smith, "but"—

"Very well," said the squirrel; "then when *I* jump, I fly."

"But you haven't got wings," said Tommy Smith. He knew he was right, but he didn't know how to prove it.

"That makes it all the more clever of me," said the squirrel. "It is easy enough to fly if you have wings, but very difficult indeed if you haven't. But we squirrels are a clever family, and can do anything. Why, one of us is called the 'Flying Squirrel,' you know; and why should he be called a flying squirrel if he can't fly? Not fly? Why, look here!—look here!—look here!"—and at each "look here!" the squirrel was in a different tree, and still he went on jumping, or flying (which do *you* think it was?), from one to another, until very soon he was quite out of sight.

And he never came back—at least not whilst Tommy Smith was there. I think he must have come back at *some* time or other, to sit in his little summer-house again with his wife and children. But Tommy Smith had not time enough to wait for him; so, as soon as he was sure that he was really gone, he walked away to his friend the woodpigeon.

CHAPTER XI.

THE BARN-OWL

*In at Tommy Smith's window the owl has a peep;
He talks to him wisely, and leaves him asleep."*

IT was just the very exact time for a little boy like Tommy Smith to have been in bed for about five minutes (your mother will know *what* time it was); so, of course, he *had* been in bed for about five minutes, and he wasn't asleep yet. It was a beautiful night, the window was open a little at the top, and Tommy Smith was looking through it, right away to where the moon and the stars were shining. All at once a great white bird flitted across the window—so silently!—without making any noise at all. Most birds, you know, make a swishing with their wings, which you can hear when you are close to them (sometimes when a good way off too, like the peewit), but this bird made none at all.

"Oh!" cried Tommy Smith, "whatever was that?" As he said this, the great white bird flew back again, but — just fancy!—instead of passing by the window as it did before, it flew up on to it, and sat with its head inside the room, looking at Tommy Smith. "Oh, who are you?" said Tommy Smith. And yet he knew quite well that it was an owl. No other bird could have such great, round eyes, and such a funny wise-looking face.

The owl sat looking at Tommy Smith for a little while, and then he said in a very wise tone of voice, "Guess who I am."

"I think you are the owl," said Tommy Smith.

"That is right," said the owl. "But what kind of owl do you think I am?"

"Oh," said Tommy Smith, "I suppose you are the owl that says 'Tu whit, tu whoo.'"

"I am *not*," said the owl very decisively. "I have never said anything so absurd in the whole of my life. Why, what does it mean? Nothing, *I* should say. It has simply *no* meaning. What I *do* say is 'Shrirr-r-r-r,' which is very different, is it not now?"

"Yes," said Tommy Smith, "it is very *different*, but"—

"Of course it is," said the owl; "when I

say *that*, I feel that I am making a sensible remark."

Tommy Smith didn't think that "shrirr-r-r-r" was a *much* more sensible remark than "tu whit, tu whoo," but he thought he had better not say so, as the owl spoke so positively.

"There are a great many different kinds of owls in the world, you know," the barn-owl continued. "Some are very large, as large as an eagle, and others are a good deal smaller than I am. Here, in England, there are three kinds,—the wood-owl, the tawny owl (I can't answer for what *they* say), and the barn-owl. Now *I*, thank goodness, am a barn-owl. I must ask you to remember that, because, naturally, I shouldn't like to be mistaken for one of the others."

"Oh, I'm sure I shall remember it," said Tommy Smith, "because"—

"Never mind saying why," said the owl, "it would take too long. Well, and were you surprised to see me?"

"Oh yes, I was a little," said Tommy Smith. "I just looked up, and I saw a great white thing going past the window."

"I suppose I looked white to you," said

the owl; "but that is because *you* are not nocturnal, as I am. But, if you were an owl, like me, you would see that I am not really white. At anyrate, there is more of me that isn't white, than that is. My face is white, I know,—these beautiful, soft, silky feathers that make two circles round my fine dark eyes,— my face-discs they are called (what a pity you can't see them better!), *they* are white, and very handsome they look. I am very proud of them, for I am the only owl in England that has them. But, after all, my face, though it is beautiful, is only a small part of me. My back, which is much larger, is not white at all, but a light reddish yellow. There, now you get the moonlight on it nicely. Such pretty, delicate colouring. What a pity you are not nocturnal! Then, even my breast is not quite white. It has some very pretty grey tints about it. And yet I am called the 'white owl,' as well as the 'barn-owl,' and often that name is put first in books. It is very annoying. The barn-owl is a good sensible name; for I do know something about barns, and I am very fond of catching the mice that live in them. But why should I be called white, when

THE BARN-OWL

I have such pretty colours? It is one of my grievances. You know I have a good many grievances."

"Have you?" said Tommy Smith. (He knew what a grievance was; one of those things that ought never to be made out of anything.)

"Yes," said the owl; "and do you know what I do with them?"

"No," said Tommy Smith. He didn't *quite* understand what the owl meant.

"Well," said the owl—"mind, I'm going to say something very wise now (you know I'm an owl),—I put up with them."

"Oh!" said Tommy Smith.

"Yes," said the owl. "It will take you a very long time to find out what a wise remark that was. *You* couldn't have made it, you know; I mean, of course, with the proper expression. I couldn't myself *once*, when I was only a young owl, but now that I am grown up, and have a wife and family to assist me, I can."

"Oh yes," said Tommy Smith. (It was all he could think of to say.)

"You've no idea," the owl went on, "what a time it takes one to make *some* remarks properly. Now take, for instance, the one, 'It's a sad world!' It *seems* very easy, but even if you were to repeat it a hundred times a day for the next fortnight, you wouldn't be able to say it in the way it ought to be said—like this," and the owl snapped his beak, and said it again. "*That* sounds *convincing*," he remarked; "but as for a little boy saying it in *that* way,—no, no."

"Is it so *very* difficult," said Tommy Smith.

"Well, it wants help," said the owl; "that's the principal thing. If you were left to yourself, you'd never manage it; but first one person helps you, and then another, until at last—after a good many years, you know—you get into the way of it. It's like shrugging one's shoulders. It takes one half a lifetime to do *that—well*."

"Does it?" said Tommy Smith.

"Ask your father," said the owl; "only you mustn't expect him to make such a wise answer as I should, because, of course, he isn't an owl, like me."

Tommy Smith didn't think the owl had said anything so *very* wise, but he had used a word twice which he didn't know the meaning of, and so he said, "Please, Mr. Owl, what does being 'nocturnal' mean?"

"To be nocturnal," said the owl, "is to wake up and see at night, and go to bed in the daytime, which is what we owls do."

"Oh yes, I know," said Tommy Smith; "and if an owl ever *does* come out in the daytime, a lot of little birds fly after him and"—

"Yes," said the owl. "It is very grand, is it not, to be attended in that way? Common birds have to fly about by themselves, but, of course, when one is a great owl, it is natural that people should make a fuss about one."

"But, Mr. Owl," said Tommy Smith (he really couldn't help saying this, though he was afraid the owl might be angry), "don't the little birds fly after you because they don't like you, and"—

"Dear, dear!" said the owl, "what funny notions little boys do get into their heads. Not like me, don't they? That is very ungrateful of them, because *I* like *them* very much. Sometimes I like them almost as much as a mouse, you know. But, after all, what does it matter whether they like me or not? The important thing is to have a retinue, all the rest is of no consequence. Why do you suppose"— The owl stopped all of a sudden, as if he had just thought of something, and then he said, "But, perhaps, hearing so many wise things, one after the other, in such a short time, may be bad for you,—too much strain on the brain, you know. What do you think?"

"Oh, I don't think it will do me any harm," said Tommy Smith."

"Very well," said the owl; "in the cool of the night, perhaps, it may not, but I wouldn't answer for it in the daytime, if the sun was at all hot. Well, now do you suppose that if all the people in the world who had retinues were to know what their retinues thought about them, they would be any the happier for it?"

"I don't know," said Tommy Smith.

"Well," said the owl (I really cannot tell you how wise he looked as he said this), "*I do.*"

"But what *is* a retinue?" asked Tommy Smith.

"Oh dear," said the owl, "I have been forgetting that I am a wise owl, and that you are only a little boy who doesn't know long words. A retinue is an *entourage,* you know, and "—

"But I don't know what that word means either," said Tommy Smith (and, indeed, he thought it was rather a more difficult one than the other).

"Oh dear," said the owl, "I am forgetting again. Why, when there are a lot of little birds, who fly round you and twitter whenever you come out and show yourself, that is what I call having a retinue or an *entourage*; and, depend upon it, it is a very grand thing to have. The more birds there are to twitter about you, the grander bird *you* are. But it doesn't so much matter *what* they twitter, and as for what they *think,* you had better know nothing at all about *that.*"

It was all very well for the owl to talk in this very wise way, but Tommy Smith felt sure that the little birds didn't like him at all, and only flew round him to annoy him when he happened to come out in the daytime. And he didn't think it was such a very grand thing to have a retinue like that. "They would peck at him too, I daresay, if they weren't afraid," he said to himself; "and no wonder, if he eats them." But he wasn't quite sure whether the owl did this or not, so he thought he had better ask him before feeling angry with him.

"*Do* you eat the little birds, Mr. Owl?" he said.

"Not very often," the owl answered. "The fact is, I don't so *very* much care about them. Only, sometimes, when I want a change of diet, or if they happen to get in my way, I like to try them. They can't complain of *that*, you know."

"Why not?" said Tommy Smith.

"They haven't time," said the owl. "You see, I catch them asleep, and by the time they wake up, they've been eaten."

"I think it's a great *shame*," said Tommy Smith; "and I think you're a *wicked* bird to do it. You ought to be shot for doing such things, and when I am grown up, and have a gun"—

"Wait a bit," said the owl. "Do you know what you would be doing if you were to shoot me? Why, you would be shooting the most useful bird in the whole country. You wouldn't want to do *that*, I suppose?"

THE BARN-OWL

Tommy Smith didn't quite know what to say to this. "Of course, if you really *are* very useful," he began—

"Well, if you were a farmer," the owl went on, "I don't suppose you would like to have all your corn, and wheat, and hay, and everything eaten up by rats and mice, would you?"

"Oh no," said Tommy Smith.

"That is what would happen, though, if it wasn't for me," said the owl. "You see, *I* eat the rats and mice. They are my proper food, especially the mice. A full-grown rat is rather large for me—too large to swallow whole, at anyrate; and I like to swallow things whole if I can. But the mice and the young rats are just the right size, and you've no idea what a lot of them I eat. I have a very good appetite, I can tell you, and so have my children. Of course, I have to feed them as well as myself, so there is plenty of work for me to do. Every night I fly round the fields and farmyards, and when I see a mouse, or a rat, or a mole, or a shrew-mouse, down I pounce upon it. Now think how many owls there are all over the country, and think what thousands and thousands of rats and mice they must catch every night, and then think what a lot of good they must do. Or, here is another way. Think how many rats and mice there are even now, although there are so many owls to catch them, and think how much harm they do, and think how many more there would be, and how much more harm they would do if there were no owls to catch them. That is a lot of thinking is it not? Well, have you thought of it all?"

"I've tried to," said Tommy Smith.

"It's difficult, isn't it?" said the owl. "It's all very well to say 'think,' but the fact is, you *can't* think what a useful bird an owl is—and especially a barn-owl. But, perhaps, you don't believe me."

"Oh yes, I do," said Tommy Smith. "I always thought that owls killed rats and mice."

"You can prove it, if you like," said the owl, "and I'll tell you how. I told you that I liked to swallow animals whole, so, of course, everything goes down—fur, bones, feathers (if it does happen to be a bird), and all. But I can't be expected to digest such things as that, so I have to get rid of them in some way or other. Well,

THE BARN-OWL

what do I do? Why, I bring them all up again in pellets about the size and shape of a potato."

"Oh, but potatoes are of different sizes and shapes," said Tommy Smith.

"*I* mean a smallish-sized oblong potato," said the owl. "That is what my pellets look like, only they are of a greyish sort of colour. Sometimes they are quite silvery."

"How funny!" said Tommy Smith.

"How pretty, I suppose you mean," said the owl. "Yes, they *are* pretty. Now, if you look about under the trees in the fields where I have been sitting, you will see these pretty pellets of mine lying on the grass. Pick them up and pull them to pieces, and you will find that they are nothing but the fur, and skulls, and bones of mice, and shrew-mice, and young rats. Sometimes the skull and beak of a bird will be there, and then it will almost always be a sparrow's. Sparrows are a nuisance, you know, because there are too many of them. But, as for mice, there will be three or four of them in every pellet (you can count them by the skulls), and you know what a nuisance *they* are. Let anyone who is not quite sure whether I am a useful bird or not look at my pellets. Then he'll know, and if he shoots me after that, he must either be very stupid, or very wicked, or both. Well, do you still mean to shoot me when you grow up?"

"Oh no," said Tommy Smith, "I never will, now that I know how useful you are, and what a lot of good you do."

The owl looked very pleased at this, so Tommy Smith thought he would take the opportunity to ask his advice about something which had been puzzling him a good deal. "Please, Mr. Owl," he said, "I promised the rat not to kill him any more. But, if rats and mice do such a lot of harm, oughtn't I to kill them whenever I can?"

"Certainly not," said the owl. "A little boy should be kind to animals, and not trouble his head about anything else. No, no; be kind to animals and leave the rats and mice to *me*." That was the wise owl's advice to Tommy Smith, and *I* think it was very good advice.

"Where do you live, Mr. Owl?" (that was the next question that Tommy Smith asked). "I suppose it is in the woods."

"No," the owl answered. "Barn-owls do not live in the woods. The tawny-owls and the wood-owls do. Woods are good enough for them, but we like to have more comfortable surroundings We don't object to trees, of course. A nice hollow tree is a great comfort, and I, for one, could not do without it. But it must be within a reasonable distance of a village, and the closer it is to a church, the better I like it."

"Do you, Mr. Owl," said Tommy Smith.

"Yes," said the owl. "I don't mind how far I am from a railway station or even a post office, but the church *must* be near."

"I suppose you like to sit in the tower, Mr. Owl," said Tommy Smith.

"I should think so," said the owl; "the belfry is there, you know, and I am so fond of that. It is so nice to sit in one's belfry and think of one's barns, and farms, and haystacks. And then, when the bells ring, you can't think what fun that is —especially on the first day of January when they ring in the New Year. I get quite excited then, and I give a scream, and throw myself off the old tower, and fly round it, and whoop and shriek until I seem to be one of the mad bells myself. For they *are* mad then, you know. They go mad once every year—on New Year's day. People come out to listen sometimes. They look up into the air, and say, 'Hark! There they go. It is the New Year now. They are ringing it in.' Then all at once the bells stop ringing, and it is all over; the New Year has been rung in. But what there is new about it is more than *I* can say, wise as I am. It all seems to go on just the same as before, and sometimes I wonder what all the fuss has been about. I have never been able to see any difference myself between the last minute of the thirty-first of December and the first minute of the first of January. On a cold rainy night especially, they seem very much alike. But, of course, there must *be* a difference, or the bells wouldn't ring as they do."

"Oh, they ring because it's the new year, Mr. Owl," said Tommy Smith.

"Yes, that's it," said the owl; "but I should never have found it out without them."

Tommy Smith began to think that the owl couldn't be so *very* wise after all, or surely he would have known the difference between the old year and the new year. He was going to explain it to him thoroughly, but he was getting rather sleepy by this time, and it is difficult to explain things when one is sleepy.

So he didn't, and the owl went on with, "Oh yes, we love churches, we owls do. We have our nests there, you know, and we could not find a safer place to make them in. Anywhere else we might be disturbed and rudely treated, for people are not nearly so polite to us as they ought to be. But we are always safe in a church, for no one would be so wicked as to annoy us there. Besides, a church is a wonderful place to hide in. People pass by it, and come into it, and sit down and go out again, without having any idea that we are there, and have been there all the time. They never think of that."

"What part of the church do you build your nest in, Mr. Owl?" said Tommy Smith.

"Oh, that is in the belfry too," said the owl. "The belfry is my part of the church. I think it must have been built for me, it suits me so well. I am called the belfry-owl sometimes, and that is a very good name for me too. But now don't ask me any more questions, because you are getting sleepy, and I have something to tell you before you go to sleep."

And then the owl told all about the grand meeting that the animals had held in the woods, and all that they had said to each other, and what they had decided to do to try and make Tommy Smith a better boy to animals, and how, at first, they had wanted to hurt him (or even to kill him), because they were so angry with him, until the owl had persuaded them not to. It was all the wise owl's doing. *He* knew that the best way to make a little boy kind to animals was to teach him something about them; and who could teach him so well as the animals themselves?

CHAPTER XII.

THE LEAVE-TAKING

*"All 'Tommy Smith's Animals' take leave with joy,
For they know Tommy Smith is a different boy."*

WHEN Tommy Smith had gone to sleep, the owl flew away, and he flew to the same place where he had met the other animals before, and found them all there again waiting for him (of course, it had been arranged). Then all the animals began to tell each other about the conversations they had had with Tommy Smith, and what a very much better boy he had become. They were all so glad; and, of course, they all thanked the owl, because it had been his idea.

Then the owl thanked all the animals for thanking *him*, and he said that it *was* his idea, but that it might just as well have been the idea of any other animal there, and he wished that it *had* been, because, *then*, he could have called it clever, but *now*, of course, he couldn't, for *that* would be praising himself,—which would *never* do. You see, he wanted to be modest. One ought always to be modest when one makes a speech. And now (the owl said) he was quite sure that Tommy Smith would never be unkind to animals any more as long as he lived, because, just before he flew away, he had asked him to promise that he wouldn't. But Tommy Smith had just gone off to sleep then, and so he had had to promise it in his sleep. "And, you know," said the owl, "that when a promise is made in *that* way, it is always kept." Then all the animals clapped their—well, whatever they could clap, and said "Hurrah!" and the meeting broke up.

And the owl was right. As Tommy Smith grew older, and became a big boy, he found that animals did not talk to him any more in the way they used to do. It seemed as if they only cared to talk to *little* boys or girls. But there was one way of having conversations with them, which he got to like better and better, and that was to go out into the woods and fields and watch what they were doing. He soon found that that was quite as interesting as really talking to them. In fact, it *was* talking to them in another kind of way, for they kept telling him all about themselves, only without speaking. And the more Tommy Smith learnt about them, the more he liked them, until the animals became his very best friends. Of course, one is never unkind to one's very best friends, and, besides, Tommy Smith had given the owl a promise—in his sleep.

www.ingramcontent.com/pod-product-compliance
Ingram Content Group UK Ltd.
Pitfield, Milton Keynes, MK11 3LW, UK
UKHW042003230426
12048UKWH00009B/523